The *Visitor* Series

The Visitor Has a Ball

Book 6 by Betty Thomason Owens

Write Integrity Press

The Visitor Has a Ball
Copyright: ©2023 Betty Thomason Owens

ISBN: 978-1-951602-16-1

Published by Pursued Books: an imprint of
P Write Integrity Press
PO Box
Dallas, TX 75370

Printed in the United States of America.

Dedication

To Mom & Dad

Contents

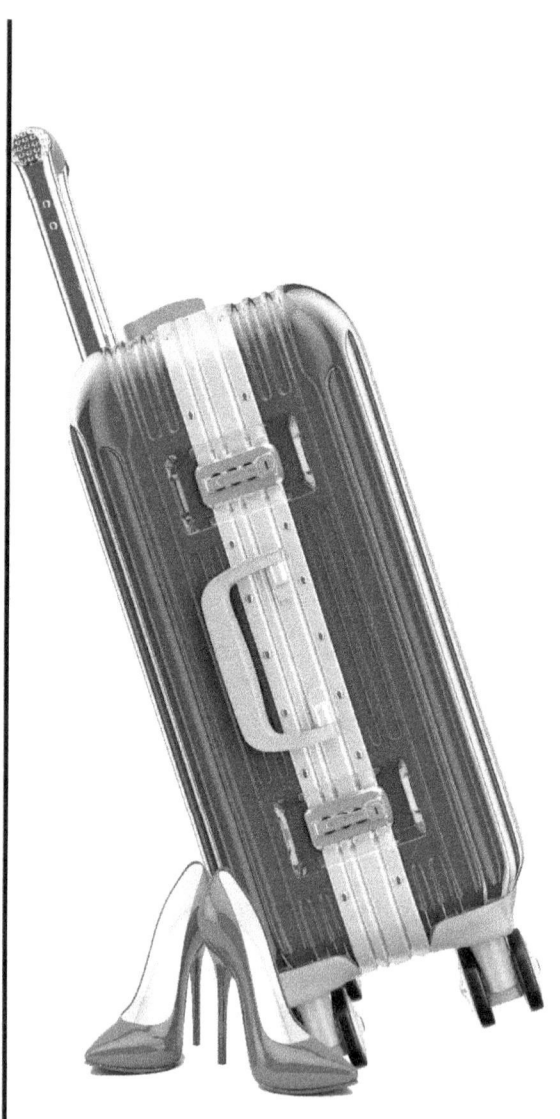

Chapter One

The Mahogany Box

Samantha Carr stood at her mother's front door talking to herself, or rather to her reflection in the sidelight. "I'm twenty-three years old. A college graduate with a great job. Why do my knees turn to jelly when I have to face Mom?" With a quick skyward glance, she whispered a prayer. "Father, may I be a help and not a hindrance to my mother."

She flipped open the lid of the wall-mounted mailbox and grabbed the envelopes stuffed in there. Might as well make herself useful. After one last deep breath, she turned the key in the lock and entered.

Stagnant air struck her in the face. *Really?* Samantha bolted the door, added the mail to the pile on the foyer table, and dropped the keys in her purse. "Mom?"

She wandered toward the kitchen. Well, at least it was spotless. The table held two place settings and a photo in a ceramic frame of Mom and Dad, celebrating their twenty-fifth anniversary. Their last. Dad passed away two months later.

Samantha stepped to the kitchen stairs. "Mom, are you up there?"

A soft thud was followed by muffled footsteps.

Samantha frowned. Feet clad in fuzzy slippers, no doubt. She hurried up the stairs, almost tripping over Bob the Cat as he made a beeline for the kitchen. "Mom?"

"Oh, dear." Mom stood in her bedroom doorway, still in her nightgown and aforementioned footwear. "Oh, dear. I had no idea it was so late. I'm sorry."

"Mom, it's almost ten o'clock. We have only a few hours to get the house ready."

Mom turned her back and shuffled toward her closet. "I wish you hadn't invited her to stay here. What were you thinking? You know how it is for me these days."

Samantha arched a brow. Her mother's present condition had prompted Samantha's invitation. "You haven't seen Aunt Connie since . . ." She stopped herself before completing the thought—Dad's funeral.

With a loud sigh, Mom plopped on her unmade bed. She chewed the inside of her cheek and rubbed her arms. "Exactly. She'll expect things to be normal." She pushed trembling fingers through her tousled, gray locks and gave another sigh.

Samantha sat next to her mother and took hold of her hand. "Can you make yourself presentable, Mom? I'll take care of everything else."

Mom stared straight ahead.

Blinking back tears, Samantha rose and stepped into the walk-in closet still shared by Dad's clothing. Her mother refused to part with anything. Samantha found an appropriate dress and held it up for approval.

Mom shook her head. "Not a dress. I'm not ready for that."

Rolling her eyes, Samantha replaced the dress with a pair of navy slacks and a lavender button-up blouse.

"Fine." Mom pushed up from the bed. "Lay them here. I'll clean up and see if I can make sense out of my hair."

"You should have kept the appointment I made for you."

No reply. At least she went into the bathroom and closed the door. A moment later, Samantha heard water running. Good sign.

While upstairs, Samantha grabbed the vacuum from the linen closet and went to work in the guest room. It had not been used for quite some time. She stripped the bed and replaced the linens, dusted, and then finished with the vacuum. The attached bathroom only needed a good once over with a damp rag and disinfectant.

Samantha's childhood bedroom looked fine, except for the dust. She shook her head. Mom had always been such a stickler about cleaning. Samantha never realized how dependent on Dad her mother had become until his death. Losing him had left her helpless.

When Samantha found out Aunt Connie would be coming in to organize a fundraising gala for the *Sally Ingram Home of the Innocents*, she had wanted to take full advantage of the opportunity.

No matter how much Mom protested, she loved her baby sister.

Aunt Connie was a strong and independent businesswoman who had taken over the reins of the Wright Foundation when Samantha's grandparents retired. Hopefully, she could wield her influence and persuade Mom to leave the house. Get involved in life again.

Samantha used a sneakered foot to shove the heavy vacuum back into place in the upstairs closet. There was another one downstairs in the laundry room. That would be her next stop.

On the way, she opened the windows wide. It was a beautiful day, and this old house needed fresh air. At least the landscaping was immaculate, though the lawn could use a trim. Mom had mentioned she had hired a landscaper to take care of it. The foyer and living room done, Samantha switched off the vacuum. She gave the wood furnishings a quick polish. When she heard Mom in the kitchen, she joined her there.

"I've put coffee on. I figured you could use a break about now." She filled the cream pitcher and set it on a tray. "I usually have my morning coffee in the Florida room."

"That's a nice habit." Samantha set two cups on the tray and then checked her phone. Nearly noon. She bit back a comment about the lateness of the hour and followed Mom.

Always impressive, the ample Florida room had somehow escaped the house dust. Several varieties of tall plants stood expertly grouped among white, wicker furniture. Red and orange hibiscus blooms offset the dark green leaves.

Throw pillows in bright colors that matched the blooms adorned a tan couch. Lowering herself onto the cushy sofa, Samantha drew in a breath of sweet-scented air.

Mom passed her a cup of coffee.

Samantha added cream and stirred. "When you told me you'd made changes to this room, I had no idea they were so extensive. It's lovely."

Mom smoothed one of the pillows before answering. "Fresh paint, new plants and throw pillows, those are the only changes. I needed a place to relax, away from the rest of the house."

"It's like a sanctuary out here. It must have been

a lot of work. Did you order these plants?"

"My landscaper drew up the design." She picked at the hem of her blouse. "He tends to it weekly."

Was she embarrassed? Wait. If he tended to the indoor plants, he would be coming inside. She eyed Mom's face. Was this landscaper an older gentleman? Someone of interest?

Mom met Samantha's gaze. "He's a young man. Around your age."

Huh. Should have known better than to hope for such a thing.

Samantha glanced at her phone again. Only a couple of hours until Aunt Connie's arrival. "Well, I need to get back to work. I don't want you to worry about anything."

Mom sat forward. "What about dinner? I don't have much."

"I've got that covered. Aunt Connie wanted to take us out tonight. I put her off. A friend of mine owns that new restaurant over on Main. She's sending something scrumptious."

Mom frowned. "I haven't had much of an appetite."

Samantha caressed her mom's cheek. "I know that. It will be all right. You'll see. Just rest."

She left Mom half reclining on the sofa and headed to the front of the house. The next project would be a difficult one.

In front of Dad's office door, she hesitated. It was closed, of course. Mom would not go in there.

As she pushed open the door, the smell almost knocked her down. What was that? Rotten eggs?

She crossed to the window and reached for the latch. It was unlocked. Odd. Mom would never leave a window unlocked. At least, not on purpose.

Mom must have been in here at some point and left the latch open. Making a mental note to remind her about it, Samantha moved to the second window and raised it.

At that moment, an engine revved outside. She peeked through the screen and noticed a man on a zero-turn mower, cutting a swath across the lawn. As he moved out of her line of vision, something on the side porch caught Samantha's notice. A large, reddish-gold dog lay in the sunshine, quite at ease, as though it belonged there.

She returned to the task at hand, determined to find the source of that revolting odor.

A bowl of something sat near the edge of the desk. The container itself was white plastic, with a green circle on the side. Samantha covered her nose and mouth with her hand. Whatever it had once been was now covered with mold and completely unrecognizable. She pulled the empty garbage bag from the can beside the desk, set the offensive thing in it and tied it off. Then she placed it in another garbage bag and tied that one. She set the doubled bag in the hall until she had finished cleaning.

Once that was gone, the smell improved a little, but she was curious. It could not have been left there by Dad. It would have been dried up by now. She shook her head to clear her mind and returned to the desk.

First things first. She gathered papers into stacks and set them carefully inside the top left drawer. At some point, she would need to go through those but not now. Time was at a premium.

Dust the furniture and vacuum.

Dad used to say that staying on task was easier if you talked your way through it. Samantha smiled at the memory of Dad mumbling to himself as he worked.

After running the vacuum, she would—wait. She stood back and examined the desk. Something was missing. A large rectangle of lighter dust on the right side of the desk confirmed it. Dad's mahogany box had stood there all her life. He had been very protective of it and always kept it locked.

Now the box was gone.

The mower outside filled the room with noise and the smell of freshly mowed grass. Samantha covered her ears. She had to think.

No, she needed to find Mom.

Chapter Two

Faux Paw

Samantha found her mother right where she'd left her, reclining on the sofa in the Florida Room.

Bob lay on her lap, licking his paw.

"Mom, what happened to Dad's mahogany box?"

Mom's eyes widened. "It's not on his desk?"

Samantha shook her head. "No, and the office window was unlocked."

Mom sat forward.

Bob jumped down and scowled at Samantha.

Easing both feet onto the floor, Mom scooted to the edge of the sofa. "I haven't been in there since before your father . . ."

"I know." Samantha held out her hand. "Come

and see."

A deep furrow creased Mom's forehead. "I—I don't think I can."

Samantha dropped her hand. It had been Dad's sanctuary, of sorts. If he was home, he was in his office. "Mom, it's been eighteen months."

Her brown eyes large and pain-filled, Mom could only whisper. "I'm sorry. I can't." She rose and shuffled toward the stairs. "I have to lie down."

Samantha gave a loud sigh and gazed at the ceiling. Her mother needed professional help, but there was something more urgent to deal with first. She grabbed her phone and called 911.

After reporting the burglary, Samantha opened the side door, intending to check for exterior signs of a break-in. She had forgotten about the dog until the moment it lifted its shiny head and thumped a fringed tail.

The creature didn't seem dangerous. As she stepped out onto the porch, its mouth dropped open into what looked like a smile.

Samantha offered her hand. "Hello, doggy."

The dog sniffed her hand but held its position.

Where was its master? Maybe he had ordered

the dog to stay. If so, this was a very obedient animal.

Sliding past, Samantha dashed down the steps and strode toward the office windows that took up the northwest corner of the house. Particularly the window that she'd found unlocked.

This side of the house was adorned with azalea bushes, all magenta, Mom's favorite color. In spring, it was a joy to behold. Most of the blooms had fallen away and the bushes appeared well trimmed.

Recently. *Hmmm.*

She arched a brow at the thought. What about the landscaper? Mom said he took care of the plants in the Florida room. So, he would have access to the house. If so, maybe he entered the office from inside and then left with the box through the window. That would explain why the window had been unlocked.

She propped her fists on her hips and peered at the house. A tallish person could easily reach the window, push it open, and climb inside, or crawl out and pull it closed afterward.

How tall was the landscaper?

Wait. She stepped closer. Something was

different about that window. What was it?

The screen was missing. How had she not noticed that? She replayed her actions in the office. When she had discovered it was unlocked, she hadn't opened that one, but moved on to the other.

Maybe whoever broke in tossed the screen behind the bushes. Dropping into a crouch, she peered beneath the shrubs. That didn't work, so she got down on her hands and knees. Her head was almost perpendicular to the ground when she detected movement to her right. Had the dog followed her?

She sat back on her heels and looked up.

A man stood several feet away, an amused look on his face. "Can I help you with something?"

Samantha pushed up from the ground and dusted off her jeans. "I was looking for, um, who are you?"

"Drew Lindner. I work for Mrs. Carr."

The landscaper. The one who was responsible for trimming these bushes.

"The screen is missing from the office window. You wouldn't know anything about that would you?"

He looked toward the house. "First I've noticed."

"Really? Well, someone broke into the office and stole something quite valuable. Would you know anything about that?"

Drew leveled his gaze at her.

Samantha bit down on her lower lip as warmth rushed into her cheeks.

He stepped closer. "Are you accusing me?" His nostrils flared. His eyes went all flinty.

Whoa. Now that she'd had a better view of his face, she wavered. He didn't look the part of a petty thief. In fact, he was quite good-looking. She shook her head. Why had she spoken so hastily? Classic Samantha. "I . . . I'm sorry. I don't know why I said that."

The dog barked.

Drew held up his hand and took a backward step. "Stay, Porter."

The dog sat and then lay down again but kept his head up, watching Samantha.

She grimaced. "Can we start over?" She thrust her right hand forward. "I'm Samantha Carr."

He hesitated before grasping her hand. "I know.

I recognized you from your pictures. Now, if you'll excuse me, I've got work to do."

She blew out a breath as he stalked away. He was still mad. And tall. Very tall. *Ugh.* She was doing it again. There was no good reason for her to suspect him. Except that he was here. And tall. Those weren't good reasons. She was still mentally rehashing her faux pas when a police cruiser pulled in front of the house and parked.

Samantha rushed to intercept. She didn't want anyone ringing the bell and disturbing Mom.

Two men approached the front door as Samantha rounded the corner—one in uniform, the other in gray slacks and white shirt, open at the collar—a detective? "Hi, I'm Samantha Carr, the owner's daughter. I'm the one who called it in. Thank you for coming." She tried to open the door and then remembered she had not come out that way and her key was inside. "I'll go around and open it."

Trotting back to the side porch, Samantha steeled herself for another encounter with Drew, but he and the dog had both disappeared. She could still hear the mower, though, so apparently, he hadn't gone far.

She rushed inside to admit the policemen. "I'm so sorry for the delay. The office is right this way." Great, now she was rhyming.

Detective Tuttle introduced himself. He stood in front of the screenless window. "You're certain there was a screen on this window?"

"Yes, there are screens on all the windows."

Outside, the other cop moved past, examining the bushes.

Pad and pen in hand, Tuttle wrote as Samantha listed the items Dad kept in the box. He leaned over the desk. "It does appear that something had been here at one time. Are you sure it wasn't moved, maybe stored in another location?"

Samantha blew out a breath. "My mother hasn't been in here since Dad's passing. I'm the only other family member, and I've been in here once in the last eighteen months, the day after he died. The box was on the desk then."

Tuttle scratched his head. "Did you open the box at that time, make sure everything that should be in there, was? The, um . . ." He referred back to the list he'd written earlier. "A packet of old letters, various birthday cards, a stack of photos, some silver coins, and a baseball, autographed by Babe Ruth." He lifted his eyes to hers.

"I . . . didn't. I'm not even sure where the key is. I really didn't touch anything, except the photo on the desk." Dad's favorite family photo, taken at the lake.

Tuttle pivoted to look at her. "What about cleaning? Does your mother have a maid or . . . a service?"

"No, she prefers to take care of things herself. Except in here, of course." She glanced around the room. *And most of the rest of the house these days.*

He made another note. "So, as far as you know, no one has been in here since your father passed?"

Hadn't she just said that? Samantha eyed the detective. "Correct. Except—" She told him about the icky food container.

He wrote something in the notepad. His brows knit together. "What did you do with that?"

Samantha scrunched her nose, stepped to the door, and pointed. "It's here, in the hallway. It's double-wrapped."

Tuttle nodded. "All right, then. I think we're finished here." He lifted the bag she'd pointed out and set it on the floor beside the desk. "You might want to leave everything as is. Your insurance company will probably want to send someone out."

He turned and strode toward the door. "If you think of anything else, give me a call." He handed Samantha a card. "In the meantime, check all the other rooms in the house, closets, garage, storage shed. Many times, you'll find that some well-meaning person has put something away and forgotten about it."

She knew he was referring to her mother. He may have seen situations like that in the past, but he didn't know Samantha's mom. She would not set foot inside the office.

Samantha trailed behind Tuttle to the front porch, where she watched as the two got into their cruiser and pulled away. Thank goodness it was a weekday. Not so many neighbors out, nosing around.

Samantha pulled her phone from her back pocket to check the time as she made her way into the office. Thank goodness Aunt Connie had reserved a rental car at the airport. One less thing to worry about.

Still, it would have been nice to have the house all ready. A shower would have been great, too, and a change of clothes. She tapped down her chagrin. Aunt Connie was always so immaculate and well-put together. As a child, Samantha had wanted to be just like her.

She located the insurance information in a file folder, along with a complete listing of everything in the house. *Thanks, Dad.*

"Are they gone?" Mom's tremulous voice sounded from the landing.

Samantha stepped toward the office door. "Yes. I have to call your insurance company and report the break-in."

"Well, I hope you're planning on being here if they have to come out. You know I can't deal with that sort of thing."

"I'm staying for a few days, Mom, remember? To help with Aunt Connie."

With a loud sigh, Mom descended the steps and shuffled toward the kitchen. "It's too much. A thief breaking in, Dad's precious box missing, and Connie coming."

Samantha fought the temptation to roll her eyes

again as she closed the office door. She had to wonder which one of those things seemed worse to her mother.

The Visitor Has a Ball

Chapter Three

High Heeler

When a silver Lexus pulled into the drive and stopped behind her Mini Cooper, Samantha trotted downstairs and out the back door. As soon as the lock clicked, Samantha opened the car door.

Aunt Connie wore jeans and a crisp, white blouse topped with a fringed denim jacket and leather shoulder bag in her signature red. She stepped out of the car in red heels that perfectly matched her purse and opened her arms. "Hello, Samantha. How is it possible, you grow more beautiful each time I see you?"

Samantha laughed as she hugged her aunt. "Flatterer." She kissed her cheek. "Thank you, Aunt Connie. I'm so glad you're here. I hope you had a good trip."

Aunt Connie stepped back. "The drive from the Louisville airport to Shelbyville took longer than my flight from Chicago to Louisville."

"A mere drive in the country compared to Chicago traffic."

Aunt Connie used the key fob to pop the trunk open. "Indeed. It is quite beautiful out here." Her gaze took in the house and grounds. "A feast for the eyes."

Samantha extracted the larger of the two suitcases.

Aunt Connie grabbed the other one, closed the trunk, and locked the car. "So how is my sister today?"

Wheeling the suitcase across the cobbled drive, Samantha kept her head down, contemplating her answer. Before they reached the stoop, she turned to her aunt. "She doesn't leave the house. Ever."

Aunt Connie paused. "That is a problem. And you have been away, I understand. How goes the new job?"

"Very well, actually, though guilt has been my constant companion."

"Oh, I've fought that battle. I assure you; it can be won. Let's get inside. We have a lot to talk about."

Samantha pushed open the door and almost stumbled over Bob, probably curious about the guest. He dashed away when Aunt Connie entered. Bob's presence usually meant Mom was not far behind. When she caught sight of her mother standing beside the sink, she stared wide-eyed. Not only had her mother combed and styled her hair, she was wearing the white turquoise necklace Dad had given her. She even wore shoes in place of the usual fluffy mules.

Her expression was more difficult to read. Samantha watched as Mom stepped forward to greet her sister.

"Connie, it's so wonderful to see you. It's been ages."

Mom's smile seemed forced at first, but as she interacted with her sister, the tension melted away. This visit was going to be a good thing.

Samantha took hold of the second suitcase handle, abandoned by her aunt, and rolled the two units into an out of the way spot beside an alcove.

She should take them upstairs, but then she'd miss the conversation between the sisters. She hadn't seen her mother so animated since . . . she couldn't remember when.

Mom poured three glasses of tea and set them on the kitchen island, along with a bowl of lemon slices. Aunt Connie pulled out a stool and took a seat. "Oh, it's so nice to relax for a few minutes."

Mom perched on a stool across from Aunt Connie.

Samantha took the seat beside her. She squeezed lemon into her tea and stirred. "What's the plan?"

Aunt Connie sipped her tea. "I hope you'll both be able to go with me in the morning, I'd like to get a look at the venue for the gala."

The crease in Mom's forehead deepened. "Oh, I don't know, we have something going on." She looked at Samantha. "Tell her what's happened."

Aunt Connie turned to gaze at Samantha. "Nothing bad, I hope?"

"I discovered that someone may have broken into Dad's office. We don't know exactly when, but his mahogany box is missing."

Aunt Connie's lips parted. "Oh, no. Were they after the baseball? Your father loved that thing. He would never have parted with that. Not on purpose."

"I know." Samantha ran a finger through the condensation on her glass. "The insurance agent is coming in the morning. But, Mom, I can handle that. You should go with Aunt Connie."

Mom huffed out a sigh. "Let's not decide right now. We haven't even allowed Connie a moment to herself." She turned to her sister. "Samantha will show you to your room. I need to speak with the landscaper before he leaves." She rose and removed a check from beneath a magnet on the fridge before heading for the Florida room.

Samantha met Aunt Connie's gaze. "We have our marching orders."

"It seems so." Good humor shining from her eyes, Aunt Connie slid from her stool, picked up her glass and purse and then followed Samantha.

Each tugging a suitcase, they made their way upstairs. Samantha filled her aunt in on the details of the alleged burglary. "It was odd, because the window was unlocked, as if someone entered the house another way and then climbed out through the window. I'm just thankful Dad was so thorough in his record-keeping. He kept an updated listing of everything in the house."

"That comes from his experience as a comptroller for a large corporation." Aunt Connie stepped into the guest room behind Samantha. "I have always loved this room."

Samantha smiled. "I'm glad. Make yourself at home. As I told you on the phone, I've ordered dinner. It should arrive around six. I hope that will be okay."

"That sounds perfect."

After seeing Aunt Connie settled in, Samantha dashed downstairs, hoping to find Mom and Drew still in the Florida room. It was empty. A quick glance outside located the two near the shrubs along the back property line, almost an acre in the distance. The fact that Mom would wander so far afield assured Samantha of her trust in Drew.

As Samantha watched, Mom pointed at a tree in the corner and then followed Drew toward it. Samantha was half tempted to trot on out there and see what they were discussing. Then she noticed the shed door standing open. This might be a good time to do what Detective Tuttle had suggested.

Inside the shed, she scanned the contents of the shelves, so neatly arranged, they reminded her of a magazine photograph. She hadn't expected such a well-organized space. It hadn't been so in Dad's lifetime.

She moved objects just enough to see behind each one, pausing every so often to make sure she could still hear Mom's and Drew's voices. If Drew caught her in here, he might think she still suspected him.

Actually, she hadn't ruled him out.

As Samantha finished the last row of shelving, a slight noise behind her sent a shock wave down her spine. She twisted about to find that dog staring at her, his mouth agape, tongue lolling out. He swished his tail and closed his mouth.

"I suppose you're wondering what I'm doing in here," Samantha whispered to the creature. She turned away from the shelf and padded slowly toward the door.

The dog moved aside for her. After stepping into the bright sunlight, Samantha stood still a moment to allow her eyes to adjust.

"Can I help you find something?"

She darted another glance at the dog and then turned around to face Drew.

He stood behind her, a pair of long-handled pruning shears in his hand.

The menacing sight took her back to the many horror films she'd seen in her youth. A few too many. "Um . . ." She shook her head and then gave a little laugh. "For a moment, I almost thought the dog had spoken. No, I . . . I was just so impressed. The shed is immaculate. Is this your handiwork?"

He stepped past her and through the shed door to hang the shears on a hook. "Your mother asked me to make sense out of the chaos in here and in the garage."

Samantha blinked. Maybe Mom wasn't so isolated after all. "Well, you've done a fine job. Thanks." As if he needed her approval.

He faced her. "She paid me well." He stepped out the door, closed it, and locked it with a key. One of many keys on a large ring he clipped to his belt.

Was there also a house key on that ring?

His attitude suggested he was still mad at her. Why did that bother her so? She had just met him.

Samantha sat on the gazebo steps, less than five feet away from the shed. The dog followed, sat at her feet, and gazed into her face. Samantha stroked the silky-smooth hair on his head and smiled. "You are a charmer."

Drew stooped to pick up a toolbox. He frowned at the dog. "Traitor."

He'd spoken it under his breath, but Samantha heard what he said. She shook her head and smiled. "I don't blame you for feeling that way. I was horrible to you."

He looked at her as though surprised she'd heard. Then he shrugged. "Porter's an emotional service dog. He senses when someone is troubled." He turned away to set the toolbox in the bed of his truck.

Samantha scratched behind the dog's ears. "I've never met a service dog." Then she sat back and looked at Drew. "Am I not supposed to interact with him?"

Drew crouched in front of them. "No, it's okay. He's not on duty." He grinned and reached forward to stroke the dog's neck. "Come on, buddy. We need to get going. One more job to do before we can head home."

Samantha watched as Drew opened the door and allowed the dog to jump up into the seat. He faced Samantha again. "I don't blame you for making an assumption. You don't know me. Your mom is a good friend of mine. So, if you need anything . . . if I can help in any way, just let me know."

Samantha pushed up from the steps. "Thank you, Drew. I appreciate that."

He tousled Porter's ears. "Porter is a good judge of people." After closing the door, he set off around the truck and climbed inside.

As he drove away, Samantha crossed the lawn to the house. Struck by a thought, she stopped before entering. If Porter was an emotional service dog, did that mean Drew had emotional problems?

Chapter Four

Candid Shot

Sunrise from her bedroom window filled Samantha with a renewed sense of peace. As a child, she had wished upon stars from this window. She'd watched the moon rise many a night, but she had seldom taken time to enjoy the scenery.

She came to attention at the sound of her aunt's voice below and trotted down the stairs.

Aunt Connie sat talking to Mom in the breakfast nook. "Your suggestion paid off, Sis. I just spoke with your friend, Nancy. She is so excited at the possibility of helping with the children."

Samantha poured herself a cup of coffee and joined them. "Nancy Briarbeck?"

Mom nodded. "I knew she'd want to help. She's

been looking for a way to get back out there after her daughter married and moved away."

Aunt Connie smiled. "Uh-huh. Empty nest syndrome."

Samantha arched her brows as she swallowed a sip of coffee. Probably best if she didn't comment on that. "Well, I'm glad to hear she'll be involved. I loved her riding lessons. She was so kind, and so gentle with the horses."

Aunt Connie jotted something in her ever-present notebook. "Glad to hear it. I'll schedule a couple of hours one morning next week. I'll copy you on the email. My contact at Home of the Innocents is thrilled about it."

Samantha checked her phone. Eight-thirty-five. "You've done all of that this morning?"

Aunt Connie smoothed her hair. "Honey, I've been up three hours already."

"She walked two miles, first thing," Mom said.

Samantha didn't miss the hint of sarcasm in her mother's voice.

Though the sisters favored in appearance, they could not be more different. Maybe it was the disparity between their ages. Mom had been in high school when Aunt Connie was born. Their parents were often away from home. From her birth, Aunt Connie had traveled with them.

Aunt Connie laid her hand on Samantha's. "We need to get going. You'll be all right here, handling the insurance agent on your own?"

Mom chimed in. "I can always stay, if you have any reservations."

Samantha smiled into her mother's hopeful expression. "I'll be fine, really. I'll have lunch ready for you when you return."

With a sigh, Mom rose and then stood looking out the window. "Well, Drew should be here later this morning. He's going to work on that mulberry tree in the back."

"Nice to know." Samantha noted her mother's drooping shoulders, very much like a surrendered animal. When her gaze dropped to Mom's feet, she covered her mouth to suppress a giggle. "Mother dear, those shoes don't go with your outfit."

Mom turned sideways to glance at her fluffy pink mules. "Oh, my goodness." She rushed upstairs to change.

Aunt Connie laughed out loud.

The look on Mom's face as they left the house stirred unexpected emotions in Samantha. She watched as her aunt backed the car around and drove away. Had she done the right thing?

Set a guard, O Lord, over my mouth; Keep watch over the door of my lips.

She almost laughed as the verses from Psalm 141 came to mind. She had been a mouthy thirteen-year-old when Mom made her memorize that passage. She pressed her palm against her chest and prayed, "I still need your guidance, Father. Help me stay out of Your way."

After cleaning the kitchen, she grabbed her phone and started up the stairs. About halfway up, the doorbell rang.

The insurance agent was an ordinary-looking woman in jeans and athletic shoes, who appeared to be in her mid-forties. A photo ID card hung on a lanyard around her neck.

The woman smiled and lifted the ID. "I'm Lucy Sims."

Samantha stepped aside. "Yes, Ms. Sims, I'm Samantha Carr. Please come in."

Ms. Sims followed Samantha to the office,

where she began at once to check the physical locations of the items listed on her clipboard. She looked at Samantha. "Did the policemen report any findings?"

Samantha shook her head. "They didn't seem too concerned about it."

Ms. Sims' expression indicated understanding. "Standard procedure, I'm afraid. There's no property damage involved, other than the missing window screen. No one was injured or threatened in the break-in." She shrugged. "Have you been able to locate the screen?"

"No, but we haven't looked very hard."

She nodded. "Okay. It's not important. If you do find it, you may want to leave it where it is and notify the police. I'm not sure if they would take the time to check for prints, but you never know."

Ms. Sims photographed the rectangle of dust on the desk. "Do you have a photo of the actual missing items?"

Samantha retrieved the insurance file and leafed through the pages to the end. "Here's a photo of the mahogany box. That's the autographed baseball beside it."

"Oh, good, and also one of the silver coins." She tugged a portable scanner from her bag and sent the pages through. "This will help. Your dad was certainly thorough."

"Yes, he was." Samantha replaced the pages in the folder.

"There were no signs of forced entry at either of the outside doors?"

Samantha nodded. "Right. We think the thief must have entered through the office window."

"Was it often left unlocked?"

"Not that I know of. But no one had been in here in some time. It was my late father's office. Mom keeps the door closed now. She prefers not to enter it."

"I see. And there was something left behind, possibly by the thief."

Samantha pointed to the bag. "It smelled to high heaven. I think it may have been food at one time."

Ms. Sims looked at the bag. "No idea what it is?"

Samantha shook her head. "It kind of smelled like rotten eggs. It was covered in mold, so . . ."

"I see. All right, Miss Carr, I'll take some

pictures of the window from outside for our files." She started to turn away.

Samantha still had unanswered questions. "What happens now? Will we be notified?"

Ms. Sims paused. "After I've emailed my report, you may hear from an adjuster. I'll let you know, either way. There is a deductible, so I can't tell you what to expect at this time."

"So, we may never recover the items or know who did this."

Ms. Sims shook her head. "Probably not. If it's important to you, you may want to hire a private detective. That can be expensive."

A quick vision of a Tom Selleck-like P.I. popped into Samantha's mind. She shook her head and followed Ms. Sims through the front door. After snapping a few pictures outside, Ms. Sims got in her car and drove away.

Samantha returned to the kitchen. She had hoped for answers but still had none. Maybe an autographed baseball meant little to local law enforcement. Didn't it matter that someone had broken into the house?

She opened her laptop and clicked on a new

browser page. How did one search for a reputable detective agency?

Wait on the Lord.

Samantha bowed her head and waited, but nothing happened. She lowered the laptop's lid. It had been a while since she'd heard that still, small voice, but the message was clear. She needed to trust God. She tapped her fingertips against the closed computer. Patience wasn't her strong suit.

She reached for her phone and navigated to the task list. Next on the agenda was a thorough search of the house. She'd planned to start in the master bedroom while Mom was away. Might as well get started. Brushing aside a heavy load of guilt, she entered her mother's room. It seemed as though time had stood still in there. The only change was the stinky cat pan in the bathroom.

Bob lay in the center of Mom's bed, flicking his fluffy tail as though irritated at her for interrupting his sleep.

She stroked his fur. "Pardon me, Your Laziness, but I have work to do."

A book on the bedside table drew her attention. She picked it up. *Haven's Flight*, by Dena

Netherton. Samantha turned it over and scanned the back cover. Interesting. Romantic suspense, Mom's favorite genre.

From there, she moved to the closet. She had just completed her search when a knock sounded downstairs.

As she descended the steps, she listened for another knock. Which door?

No one stood at the front, so she swept past the back and then the side. Finally, she went through the Florida room to the door there.

Drew stood with his back to her, looking out at the yard. Maybe he didn't have a house key, after all.

He turned when she opened the door.

"I've finished trimming the tree. I thought your mom might want to take a look and make sure it's what she wanted."

Samantha stepped outside. "She's out with her sister. I can look at it."

He gave a little whistle, and Porter bounced around the corner of the house. "Come on, boy."

Samantha tried to keep up but Drew out-strode her. At the tree, she pulled her phone from her pocket and snapped a couple of pictures. She answered Drew's unspoken question as she hit send. "I'm texting pics to Mom for approval."

She may have also captured a candid shot of the landscaper without his knowledge.

Her phone beeped as Mom answered, *Tell him it looks wonderful. And tell him thank you. Try to be polite.*

What? Samantha wanted to roll her eyes but not while Drew watched. Instead, she nodded to him. "Mom said it looks wonderful and thank you." She tacked on a smile at the end, feeling a little bit like an emoji.

"I'm glad she approves." He stuck his hands in his pockets. "I have a lot of respect for your mother, you know. What she's been through."

Samantha kept her face averted. Had she been wearing her feelings again? She needed to practice the poker face. He shifted his stance. "I'm not trying to take advantage of her."

Porter planted himself at Samantha's feet and gazed into her eyes. Could he also sense embarrassment? She blew out a breath as she patted his head. "Apparently, your master thinks he is a mind reader."

Drew's laughter echoed through the empty backyard.

Samantha watched him behind a smile of her own. He had a nice laugh. She could like this guy. If only.

Picking up on her uneasiness, Porter snuggled closer.

She combed her fingers through the dog's hair before stepping past him. "I guess I'd better get inside. They'll be back soon, and I promised to have lunch ready." She turned to Drew. "Will you join us?"

He pushed a ball cap onto his head and smiled. "Thanks for the invitation, but I have commitments today. Maybe another time?"

"Sure." Baby steps, Samantha. Baby steps. Deal with one problem at a time.

The Visitor Has a Ball

Chapter Five

Burgled Peace

Samantha stood back and eyed her work. She had never developed cooking skills, but she could create a beautiful salad. And the fruit plate was a masterpiece.

When Mom and Aunt Connie arrived, they brought something unexpected—a jovial atmosphere. Samantha blinked. Was that her mother all chatty with Aunt Connie?

While Aunt Connie stowed her gear, Mom helped fill the glasses with fresh lemonade. "How did things go with the agent?"

Samantha shook her head. "I don't know anything yet. Ms. Sims said we might hear from an adjuster, but I'm not sure when that will be."

Carrying her glass, Mom led the way to the round dining table in the Florida room. "Oh, Samantha, this looks delicious. That fruit plate is stunning."

Aunt Connie agreed. "Well, she is an artist after all. I expect you to lend your expertise to our decor. We need a special table for the silent auction at the gala. Something that will be eye catching. A perfect project for you."

"Good idea," Mom said. "I'm sure Samantha can come up with a wonderful plan."

After blessing the food, Samantha passed a plate of thinly sliced bread. "What's the venue like?"

"Oh, it's everything I hoped for." Aunt Connie spread a bit of butter on her bread. "Plenty of space for tables and an area for dancing."

"And the best part is," Mom paused to smile, "some of the children are going to do a presentation."

The subdued joy on Mom's face clogged Samantha's throat, nearly causing her to choke. A sip of lemonade provided time to formulate an appropriate response. "That's wonderful. Everyone will love that."

"Your mother came up with the idea of a display of art created by some of the children." Aunt Connie used her napkin to dab at her lips.

This day was getting better and better. Samantha reminded herself to breathe and settle her emotions. Best not to get too hopeful, it was early yet.

Mom picked at her food and then excused herself. "I'll be in my room if you need me. I'm not used to so much activity."

Samantha glanced at Aunt Connie, who smiled.

Aunt Connie sat back. "Tell me about your job. Are you settling in well?"

"I like it, though the marketing angle is a little bit more difficult. Right now, they have me doing research. They give me a product, and I write up a detailed report. I find out what has worked and what has not."

"Are you happy with that?"

Samantha bit her lip. She wasn't but had no intention of confessing her doubts this early. "It's a learning process. I don't think I'll be doing that particular job for long."

"So, there's a future with promotion possibilities, I hope?"

Samantha preferred to evade that question. "Well, I still have a lot to learn."

Aunt Connie sipped lemonade and gave a slow nod. "That's a good attitude. So, how did you manage to get time off already? What has it been, six months?"

"Eight months, and I worked as an intern for them last summer. Of course, that didn't count toward my probationary period, which just ended a couple of weeks ago. I have a terrific boss, though, very family oriented. She encouraged me to do this, especially when I told her all about you." Samantha couldn't help smiling.

Aunt Connie gave her hand a squeeze. "Glad I could be of assistance. Let's invite her to the gala."

Samantha shrugged. "It might be too last minute."

"Maybe, but at least give her the chance to refuse. She'll appreciate that, I'm sure." She stood and carried her dishes to the sink.

When her phone rang, Aunt Connie excused herself, leaving Samantha alone with her thoughts.

The day had gone well, considering. After cleaning up and putting the food away, she reached for her laptop and emailed an invite to her boss.

Detective Tuttle called at two o'clock. "I received the photos of the missing items from your insurance agent. I can't promise anything, but I'll include them with your file."

She huffed out a sigh. His words were a pin in the balloon of her expectations. She wanted to end the call and hang up on him but that would be rude.

"I'm sorry, Miss Carr. It's just that we're spread so thin over here."

His complaint reminded her of a Tolkien quote. "Like butter scraped over too much bread."

"Exactly. Bilbo said that in one of those Ring books, I forget which."

Samantha sniffed. Had he read Tolkien, or had he only seen the movies? She forced a calm answer, *"The Fellowship of the Ring."*

"That was it." He breathed out a sigh. "I'll keep this front and center. If we hear anything, I'll call, but in most of these cases . . ."

"I know." They were short-staffed, and this was not an emergency.

Freed from the frustrating conversation, Samantha wandered into the hallway and stopped in front of the closed office. Her hand on the knob, she twisted it and pushed the door open. Stale air hit her in the face and sent an odd chill racing up her spine.

Someone had broken in here, stolen Dad's treasured box, and climbed back out again. All while Mom slept upstairs. Well, assuming it had happened at night, which it most likely had.

Just thinking about it gave Samantha the willies. She crossed to the window and double-checked the lock. She also checked the other window, just in case.

Maybe she should look into one of those alarm systems.

"Any news?" Aunt Connie asked from the doorway.

Samantha jumped. She had been so wrapped up in her thoughts, she hadn't even heard her approach. "Oh, uh . . . no. Nothing definitive."

"I see. Sorry about that. So, what's your next move? Any ideas formulating in that active young mind of yours?"

"I was just wondering if we should get an alarm

system."

Aunt Connie frowned and shook her head. "You don't want to confuse your mother. She or that mischievous cat of hers might set it off." She grinned. "Can you imagine the panic?"

Samantha giggled. "You're probably right."

Aunt Connie put an arm around Samantha's waist and drew her out of the stuffy office. "It's a little bit depressing in here. Come look at my plans and tell me what you think."

Aunt Connie's plans were coming together at light speed. Of course, she had been working on them well ahead of her arrival. Samantha scanned the drawings that detailed the locations of tables, booths, the dance floor, and the stage. They even had a contingency for overflow onto an outside patio. "I like the secret garden theme." It was Aunt Connie who had given her the book many Christmases ago.

Her aunt gave her a sideways hug. "I knew you would like it." She pointed to the largest booth marked, *Silent Auction*. "This will be your baby. You have carte blanche."

"Carte blanche? I can do a lot with that."

Visions of the aisles of a certain craft store danced through her mind.

Aunt Connie shook her head and smiled. "Within reason, dear heart. It is a charity, after all."

Samantha giggled. "Of course. I'll work on it tonight."

"After our evening meal, I hope. One of our sponsors has invited us to dinner at *The Red Lion* tonight."

"Oh, *The Red Lion*. It used to be the Science Hill Inn, but it closed during the pandemic. The owners rebranded. Great marketing ploy. I've heard it's very good. Usually packed."

When her phone pinged, Aunt Connie glanced at it and set it back down. "We have a six-thirty reservation. Tom and Beth Mitchell will meet us there."

Samantha didn't want to say it out loud, but she doubted whether Mom would go to a restaurant. "Sounds good."

"I know what you're thinking. I have already spoken with Eva Grace. I asked, but I'm not forcing her. We have plenty of time to get her out of the house if she'll go. But if that means we have dinner on our own tonight, then so be it. We can always bring her something."

"I like that plan." Samantha crossed to the fridge and opened it. "Especially since the cupboard is bare. Maybe I should head out to the grocery. Can I get you anything?"

"A carton of my favorite fizzy water, if you don't mind."

The neighborhood market bustled with activity. Samantha maneuvered a loaded cart through packed aisles before making her way to the produce section. Mom needed lemons. After struggling to open a plastic bag, she picked up a lemon and dropped it in.

"Samantha, is that you?"

She turned to greet Mom's neighbor, Mitzi Chandler. "In the flesh. It's great to see you."

"I was just wondering if I needed to check with your mother, since I knew you were home. I usually get her groceries." She pushed her cart closer, making way for other shoppers.

"Yes, she told me. Thank you so much for doing that."

Mitzi shook her head. "Eva Grace would do the same if the tables were turned. How is she this week? I hope your aunt's visit has lifted her spirits."

"It has. She even went out with Aunt Connie this morning."

Mitzi's brows arched. "Oh, my goodness. I am so happy to hear that. Maybe one day soon, I can persuade her to go shopping or out to lunch or something."

"I hope so." Samantha picked up another lemon and looked it over before adding it to the bag.

Mitzi leaned closer. "She's made such progress since Drew and Porter Wagger started working with her."

Samantha dropped another lemon in the bag. Wait—what had she said—Drew was working *with* Mom? "Porter . . . Wagger?"

"Isn't that just the cutest name? He's a wonderful dog, and so sensitive. As soon as Drew told me about him, you know, what he does and all, I knew it would be good for your mother."

Samantha twisted the top of the bag and tied a knot in it before setting it in the cart. "How thoughtful of you to do that for her."

It was the only thing Samantha could come up with to say, other than to stammer that she hadn't known anything about it, which was true, but how embarrassing was that? After ending the conversation as politely as possible, she headed for the nearest checkout.

So, Drew wasn't the one in therapy. He was the therapist.

The Visitor Has a Ball

Chapter Six

Dodging the Match

Samantha couldn't stop thinking about Mitzi's revelation. How long had this doggy therapy been going on? Maybe not long, since Mom didn't seem much better than when Samantha had last visited.

She stowed the groceries in the pantry and fridge and then joined Aunt Connie in the formal dining room where her aunt had laid out the plans for the gala.

Aunt Connie looked up when Samantha entered. "My assistant just informed me that we received twelve RSVPs today."

"That's terrific." Samantha sorted through the envelopes that were still stacked on the hall table. She found the invitation for her mom and held it up.

"Make that fourteen."

Aunt Connie chuckled, "Oh no, you two were on my list from the beginning. And I've also added thirty-two others who emailed. So far, we have a ninety-percent acceptance rate." She lifted her brows.

"I invited Uncle Paul and Teagan, and they have accepted. He plans to drive down on Saturday, in time for the event."

Even though they were less than an hour away, Samantha didn't get to see her younger cousin very often. "Sounds great. I can't wait to see them."

Both their phones trilled with a message alert. They looked at each other before checking.

When she saw who it was from, Samantha shook her head and laughed. Mom had sent them a group text.

Sorry, but I need to beg off tonight's dinner. Too tired. See you in morning.

Samantha shrugged. "Not surprised."

After sending an answer, Aunt Connie set her phone down. "We don't dare rush her. Let's just count today a victory, and let it go at that."

Samantha enjoyed the short trip through

Shelbyville's historic district to the restaurant. Not driving meant she could see the sights.

Aunt Connie slowed. "Oh, look, Samantha, a peddler's mall. Would that be a place where you could look for lost items?"

Samantha followed her aunt's gaze to what had once been a small grocery. "Maybe. I hadn't thought about it. Or pawn shops?"

"Be careful with those. Promise me you won't go by yourself. Take a friend with you. Maybe that nice young man who works for your mom."

Hah. As if she'd ask Drew. He had offered to help, but she wasn't asking. She glanced at Aunt Connie. "Don't worry. I won't go alone."

Moments later, her aunt pulled into a parking spot along Washington Street.

The Mitchells waited for them at the door. After Aunt Connie made the introductions, Mr. Mitchell ushered them inside.

The former Science Hill Inn had recently been redecorated. Its whitewashed brick walls showcased colorful equine-themed paintings. Each table held fresh flowers in crystal vases. The restaurant's bid to become a premier upscale dining establishment seemed a sure thing, in Samantha's opinion. The food surpassed her expectations.

Beyond answering a couple of questions directed toward her, Samantha listened. Aunt Connie's friends were intelligent and genuine. He was a CPA at a web design company, and his wife was a professor at a local college. Though Samantha had anticipated a dull evening, it was anything but.

As they prepared to leave, Mr. Mitchell passed his card to Samantha. "Let me know if you ever decide to relocate. We could use someone with your marketing talents and abilities."

Cutting a glance toward her aunt, Samantha pocketed the card. It couldn't hurt to have options.

"What a wonderful meal," Aunt Connie said as they walked to the car.

"The company was nice, too. I especially enjoyed Mr. Mitchell's dog stories. Which reminds me, has Mom said anything to you about Drew's dog?"

Aunt Connie glanced at Samantha over the top of the car. "No, why would she?"

"Oh. I thought . . . maybe I shouldn't say anything."

Aunt Connie unlocked the car, and they both got in. After fastening her seatbelt, she looked at Samantha. "Well, now that you brought it up, Sammie, you have to."

Samantha scowled at her. "You know I don't like that name."

She grinned. "I do know. So, what about Drew's dog? Is she frightened of it? I seem to remember she's not fond of canines."

Samantha shrugged. "She was always a cat person. But she's not frightened of him." Better to just speak the thing. "He's an emotional therapy dog."

Aunt Connie's mouth dropped open. "A therapy dog. Well, that explains a lot. I wondered what the connection was with that young man."

"Connection?"

"Yes, almost a mother-son vibe. Have you never picked up on that?"

Samantha shook her head. "No." Odd. Was she jealous? Was that weird?

Oblivious to Samantha's inner struggle, Aunt Connie kept talking. "I've heard a lot of good things about emotional therapy dogs. They provide support and help patients learn to trust." She snapped her finger and pointed to the sky. "Yes, that must be the reason she needs to be home when he's going to be there. She told me she can't be away on Thursday afternoons, because that's when her landscaper comes." She looked at Samantha. "So, she told you about him?"

Samantha sighed. "No, I ran into the next-door neighbor at the grocery this afternoon. Well, not physically ran into . . . um . . . I think you've met Mitzi?"

"I have, wonderful woman. Eva Grace said she's been a great help to her this past year."

"Yes. She and Mom have been best friends for years. Mom had been looking for a new landscaper, so, Mitzi sent him over. Of course, Mitzi knew all about his therapy work. I think she's been worried about Mom and hoped he'd be able to help her."

"Wouldn't that be something? Hmm. I wonder . . ."

Samantha eyed her aunt. "You're thinking of asking him to help with the gala, aren't you?"

Aunt Connie smiled. "Something like that. You are quite good at deduction—or is it deducing? You should put that talent to good use." She pulled into the drive and parked. "If I have any free time over the next few days, let's go check out that peddler's mall. At the very least, we may find something we can add to the auction."

Samantha released her seatbelt. "Sounds like a good plan. And I'll help by going through Mom's attic to make sure the box wasn't stowed up there."

Aunt Connie nodded. "Keep your eyes open for treasures. You never know when you may find something valuable."

Why did her aunt's typical "truism" bring Drew's face to Samantha's mind? She was uncertain but dismissed it as quickly as it had come. She did not have time to entertain pointless crushes.

By sunup, Samantha was out for a run. Exercise helped her keep in shape and cleared her mind. She needed to stay focused for the next few days.

Aunt Connie was leaving as Samantha walked back up the drive.

"I have a gazillion errands to run this morning. I'll be back around noon. Then we can head over to the venue to meet with a florist and the caterer."

"I'll be ready." It was quiet as she walked in the back door. Samantha poured herself a small glass of freshly squeezed orange juice before climbing to the third floor.

Morning sunlight streamed in through a large crescent window on the front of the house. Once upon a time, Dad had planned to turn this space into either an office or a game room. He had never quite made up his mind. And then, he had died before he'd had a chance to do either.

Samantha mopped her forehead with an old tee shirt she'd rescued from the rag pile.

Mom kept everything. The attic was proof of that.

After almost an hour and a half, Samantha gave up. No mahogany box, but she had found a number of auction-worthy items. She dusted off a rose hued Tiffany-style lamp and set it on a crate near the staircase.

Her phone alarm went off. She still needed a shower before Aunt Connie's return. As she passed by the crescent window, her gaze fell to the street below where a dark car sat next to the curb. There was something familiar about it. Something she couldn't quite put her finger on.

She dashed down the stairs, but by the time she reached the main floor, the vehicle had gone.

Mom stepped into the hallway. "Surely, you are not planning to wear your running shorts today? And you're all sweaty." She frowned and wrinkled her nose.

"I'm sorry. I lost track of time. I'll be back down in fifteen minutes, tops."

Mom sniffed. "I've heard that too many times to believe it."

Samantha gave a fake gasp before heading back up the stairs. Had Mom actually teased her?

A text from Aunt Connie gave Samantha a few extra minutes. She was dressed and ready in plenty of time. Before leaving the house, Mom tested all the doors, making sure they were locked. Samantha couldn't recall her ever doing that.

Aunt Connie whisked them to the gala venue, a white-columned, Southern Belle of a mansion known for its ties to a certain Kentucky colonel.

The caterer met them in a private dining room. Of course, chicken was on the menu in several forms. Samantha stuck with the fresh vegetables and dips, which were quite good.

The florist won Samantha's hearty approval by choosing blooms common to an English country garden. Pink and cream roses, primroses, pink and lavender delphiniums, and white hydrangeas.

"It's a bit like wedding planning, isn't it?" Aunt Connie said, with a knowing wink in Samantha's direction.

Mom fingered a flower petal. "I'm beginning to wonder if I'll ever have a chance to find out."

Samantha offered a placid smile. Let them have their fun.

"Could be sooner than you think," Aunt Connie said.

Samantha pretended she hadn't heard and stared straight ahead. Aunt Connie was the most determined person Samantha knew. If she set her mind on a thing, she would not let it go until it was accomplished.

Samantha was also determined. She must work very hard to keep any growing interest in a certain landscaper off her face and out of the conversation. Her number one priority was finding Dad's box. Sooner, rather than later.

The Visitor Has a Ball

Chapter Seven

Dog & Pony Show

There were only a few empty seats available when Samantha followed Aunt Connie and Mom into the sanctuary on Sunday morning. A young couple made room for them on the next to last pew as the song leader announced the opening hymn. Mom had timed it just right. There was no opportunity for interaction with any of her old friends.

Still, Samantha wanted to pinch herself. Was this real? She sneaked a peek at her mom who shared a hymnal with Aunt Connie. The sisters had similar facial features, but there the resemblance ended. Mom wore a billowy white blouse over a long skirt. Aunt Connie wore a cherry red business suit over a cream silk blouse. Mom wore comfortable flats. Aunt Connie stood tall in red stilettos.

Mom avoided Samantha's gaze. Chin up, eyelids lowered, she acted as though she had never missed a Sunday. Samantha wasn't fooled. A closer look revealed a slight tremble in her fingers as she fumbled for the right page.

As the congregation began to sing, Samantha joined in. "Joyful, joyful, we adore You, God of glory, Lord of love; hearts unfold like flow'rs before You, op'ning to the sun above.

"Melt the clouds of sin and sadness; drive the dark of doubt away; Giver of immortal gladness, fill us with the light of day!"

She closed her eyes for a moment and sent up a quick prayer that the words of the song would penetrate Mom's soul and replace her 'dark of doubt' with heavenly light.

As the service progressed, Samantha continued to pray that the sermon would speak to Mom's heart and give her the encouragement she needed.

The pastor's opening, "Sometimes the Lord speaks with a still, small voice," grabbed her attention and held it as he told the story of Elijah fleeing in fear and hiding in the wilderness. His words pricked her conscience over and over.

She had run away, leaving Mom alone to face that big, empty house after Dad died. And for what? A job she didn't even like with no opportunity for advancement. She frowned and chewed her lip. The house had been so empty without Dad.

The pastor stepped out from behind the podium. "Don't be tempted to run and hide. Don't give up. Look around. You are surrounded by those who believe as you do. What you're seeking so desperately is closer than you think." This led directly into his closing prayer.

Mom bumped against Samantha's arm as she slid her Bible into her bag. Samantha bit back a smile. The woman was ready to dash on signal. At the word, "Amen," she urged Samantha out of the pew.

Samantha took the rather strong hint and stepped aside. She acted as a bodyguard to discourage well-meaning friends and neighbors until Mom was in the clear.

Outside, Mom linked arms with her and almost

ran toward the parking lot. "Aunt Connie wants to say a word to the pastor. I told her we would wait in the car." She touched the button on the key fob and unlocked Aunt Connie's rented Lexus.

Samantha opened the door for Mom. "Did you enjoy the service?"

Mom set her bag on the floor next to her feet and tugged the seatbelt into place. "It was wonderful to attend in person again. It really does make a difference. And it's good to be reminded that we are not alone."

"Yeah. I liked that part, too. Sometimes we forget." She closed the door as Aunt Connie joined them.

"Sorry for the delay, but I wanted to let your pastor know how much I enjoyed his sermon."

At home, they changed into casual clothes, and ate lunch. While Mom cleaned up, Samantha helped Aunt Connie load the car for the next event, the annual *Sunday Afternoon in the Park*, hosted by Home of the Innocents.

Samantha pushed the last storage container into the trunk. "Did you know about this event when you scheduled the gala, or was it a happy coincidence?"

Great marketing, in her opinion.

Aunt Connie's eyes sparkled when she smiled. "Timing is everything, you know. When I first met with the administrator, she told me about the event. It's a great fundraiser. They have clowns, a petting zoo, inflatables, that kind of thing."

"It's like a little carnival, but without the rides."

"Oh, you've gone in the past?"

Samantha shook her head. "No, but we've driven by. It's usually well attended."

Aunt Connie closed the trunk. "So I was told." She led the way inside. "Today will be fun."

Samantha kept a watchful eye on Mom. She half-expected her to make some excuse and beg off.

Instead, she slipped on a pair of clean, white tennis shoes, applied lipstick, and picked up her purse. "Ready to go?"

The drive to the park took only ten minutes. When Aunt Connie pulled into the parking area, she came to an abrupt halt. "Well, ladies, all the trees appear to be taken. We'll have to park in the sun."

Mom patted her arm. "You're learning our ways, little sister. One might mistake you for a Kentucky native."

Aunt Connie laughed. "Yes, with a Chicago accent."

Samantha snickered as she slid from her seat. She helped Aunt Connie load the containers onto Dad's old folding hand truck. Boxes in tow, she trailed behind Mom and Aunt Connie.

They threaded their way through the crowds, past several food booths, and a pony ride.

A group of folks had already gathered beneath the pavilion. A large banner strung from pole to pole read, "Sunday Afternoon at the Park."

Aunt Connie introduced Mom and Samantha to Lisa Baxter, administrator of the children's home, and then handed Samantha the key to her car. "Would you mind bringing that last box from the trunk?"

When Samantha returned to the pavilion, she gazed in wonder. Mom wove among a group of children, talking and laughing. She even picked up one of the little girls. Samantha shook her head. "Unbelievable."

Aunt Connie leaned close. "I think she just needs to be needed."

Samantha bit her lip. She had neglected her

mother.

Aunt Connie touched Samantha's chin and made eye contact. "Don't fall into the pit of self-blame, dear. Lori and Cory have been dealing with this as well with Kimberly, and I'll tell you what I told Cory. It's not your fault. My sisters need to find their own paths. And so do you."

Samantha sighed. "I know."

A commotion outside the pavilion pulled her attention from Mom. A clutch of children oohed and awed over a new arrival—Porter Wagger. What was he doing here? And where was his master? Samantha took a few steps closer to the group.

Drew crouched amid them, talking about Porter's abilities. The dog was in his element, soon settling on one young boy on forearm crutches, who stood a little apart. Both legs held metal braces.

At first the boy cowered, but with Drew's help, gained the confidence to pet Porter.

Aunt Connie took hold of Samantha's arm. "They are wonderful with the children."

Samantha had to agree. "He has a gift."

Aunt Connie gave Samantha's arm a light squeeze. "The dog or the man?"

Samantha leveled a gaze at Aunt Connie. "Both." She wanted to stay close and maybe have a moment to visit with Drew, but her aunt put her to work. Alongside Mom, she handed out juice boxes and treats while Aunt Connie worked the crowd.

When the numbers began to dwindle, Drew stopped by their table. He greeted Samantha with a polite nod before addressing Aunt Connie. "I wanted to thank you, Miss Wright, for including Porter and me."

"It was my pleasure, Drew. I hope you made some valuable connections."

A smile boosting his appeal, he nodded. "Porter made some good friends today." His gaze rested on Samantha momentarily before he spoke to Mom. "It's good to see you out, Mrs. Carr."

"Thank you, Drew." Mom's countenance lit as Porter nuzzled her hand. She patted his head. "What a good boy you were today."

As Drew led Porter away, Aunt Connie sighed. "Such a fine young man."

Mom sighed. "Yes, he is."

Samantha kept her mouth shut but couldn't keep her gaze from following after the subject of their conversation.

The sun sat low in the sky by the time Samantha followed Aunt Connie and Mom through the back door of her home.

Bob raced across the tile floor to greet them. He threaded through Mom's ankles with fervor, nearly causing her to stumble.

Aunt Connie grabbed Mom's arm to steady her. "He seems happy to see us."

Samantha stiffened. Something was up. Bob usually ignored them. She headed straight for the office where she paused outside the door to listen. A slight noise, like the sound of paper rustling, made the hair stand up on the nape of her neck. She drew a deep breath and slowly exhaled before turning the knob.

"Meooow!"

Samantha jumped at Bob's unexpected yowl so close behind her. She listened for another moment. Silence. She opened the door and let it swing wide.

"Oh, no!" Both hands went to her mouth. The office was a shambles. Someone had broken in again.

"What is it, Samantha?" Mom's question was

followed by quick footsteps in the hall.

Samantha pulled the door closed. Her Mom shouldn't see this. "Call 911. We've had another break-in."

Chapter Eight

Double Exposure

Samantha leaned against the doorjamb.

"Another break-in?" Mom's face paled.

Aunt Connie pulled her phone from her purse as Samantha led her mother back toward the kitchen. Maybe this time the police would take it seriously.

Mom gripped Samantha's arm. "I'm so glad you're both here. What if I'd been alone?"

Samantha helped her onto the chaise lounge in the Florida room.

Bob jumped up and settled on Mom's lap.

Samantha smoothed his fur. "Good boy."

When Aunt Connie joined them, Samantha left to inspect all the rooms, paying close attention to the windows and doors. Before ascending the stairs, she held her breath and listened. Could someone still be lurking up there? Halfway up, she paused. What if there was someone up there? She needed a weapon of some sort, but what? She retreated to the mudroom and found a sturdy mop.

Wielding her weapon, she headed back upstairs. When she was satisfied there were no intruders lurking in the bedrooms, she padded into the hallway. Ahead of her, the door to the attic stairs yawned like a dark chasm. She grimaced, pushed the door closed, and then turned the deadbolt lock.

Hands still shaking, she returned the mop to the mudroom. Now what? She paused for a moment to gather her thoughts. She'd put water on for tea. She set up the tray and chose the cups. The rote movements calmed her nerves. While the kettle heated, she looked at Mom's supply of teabags and chose a lavender and chamomile variety. She poured the hot water into the carafe and carried the tray into the Florida room.

Aunt Connie sat with Mom, rubbing her back.

Samantha set the tray on the coffee table. "It doesn't look like they were anywhere other than the office, so whatever they were looking for must have been in there."

Mom grabbed a tissue and blew her nose. "There's nothing of value left. The box is already gone. What else could they possibly want?"

Aunt Connie looked at Samantha and shook her head.

When the bell rang, Samantha hurried to the front door. Two uniformed officers stood on the porch.

She moved aside. "Please, come in."

"Did you touch anything?" The first officer asked.

"No. As soon as I saw the mess, I closed the door, and we made the call."

He nodded. "We'll take a look. I'll let you know if we have any questions."

Samantha paced around the kitchen and up and down the hallway. Ten minutes after their arrival, the doorbell rang again.

Detective Tuttle greeted her. "I'm sorry, Miss Carr. I was busy when the call came in. So, you've had another break-in?"

Samantha nodded. "It seems so. Please, come in."

He stepped inside. "You know there's a full moon tonight. Looks like the perps are getting an early start."

"I've heard there's usually an uptick in emergency cases during full moons."

"I can attest to that. I've seen it too many times." He joined the other two in the office.

Samantha hung in the doorway as one of the officers filled Detective Tuttle in on the situation.

"Looks like the thief entered through the window. Broke the lock."

Detective Tuttle scanned the room. "From the disarray, I'd say the thief was looking for something in particular." He faced Samantha. "Do you have any idea what that may be?"

Samantha bit her lip and tried to think.

Aunt Connie joined her at the door. "The certificate, Samantha. Your mother thinks the same thief may have returned for the certificate of authentication—for the baseball."

Detective Tuttle tilted his head. "Was it stored in here?"

"Safe deposit box," Mom called from the other room, "at the bank."

Detective Tuttle nodded and made a note. "That's good. We'll process the scene. You may want to check that deposit box at your earliest convenience and make sure it is still there."

Aunt Connie tucked her arm in Samantha's. "Come sit with us, dear. Let the policemen do their job."

Mom and Aunt Connie sipped their tea and waited. Samantha perched on the edge of a chair, ready to jump up as soon as the policemen were finished.

Mom looked her way. "You may as well relax. I'm sure it's going to be a while."

Aunt Connie set her cup down and addressed Samantha. "I'm thinking maybe you were right about having an alarm system installed. Or at least, cameras outside. You are a bit hidden from the neighbors with all those wonderful, tall trees around."

Mom agreed. "Mitzi suggested cameras, also. I'll find out who installed them for her."

Aunt Connie looked thoughtful but made no response.

Footsteps sounded throughout the house.

Samantha relaxed a little. At least they were being thorough.

Several minutes later, Detective Tuttle stood in the doorway. "We're finished for now. Leave everything as is. If you haven't already, you'll want to give your insurance agent another call."

Samantha stood. Before she could respond, Aunt Connie spoke. "May we offer you something, officer? Tea, or coffee?"

Detective Tuttle waved it off. "No, thank you, ma'am. I need to get back to the department. We were able to lift some good prints on that window this time. We'll run them through the system and see if anything pops up."

Samantha followed him out. "Thank you, Detective Tuttle."

He paused and turned back as he neared the front door. "Prints don't necessarily mean it's a given, Miss Carr. But if this guy—uh—person has a prior, it will pop up." He started out the door. "Oh, and I overheard y'all talking about cameras. Always a good thing. Just make sure you go with a reputable company. Especially since your mother lives alone most of the time."

Samantha sighed at yet another reminder that she'd left her mother on her own. "Thanks, Detective."

Back inside, she found Aunt Connie in the office. She looked up when Samantha entered. "It's a little overwhelming, isn't it?"

"Yeah."

"Your mother called Drew. He's going to come over and make sure these windows are secure for the night."

Samantha blew out a breath. "I probably could have figured out a way to do that myself."

Aunt Connie smoothed Samantha's hair and smiled. "Let him help. He'll know just what to do."

After her aunt left the room, Samantha surveyed the damage to the office. Heavy-hearted, she lifted her phone and left a message for Lucy Sims at the insurance company.

The police said they had found two good prints, but whose were they? Drew was off the hook this time, because he had spent the afternoon at the park with them. Which led to another thought. The thief knew they were gone for the day.

Whoever this was must know about the

certificate of authentication. So, it could possibly be someone they knew. Someone who had come into contact with Dad at some point, because he had loved to show off that baseball and tell its story. And he had always included information about the certificate in his narrative.

Chapter Nine

Address the Dress

Samantha had just put away the last of the dinner dishes when a knock sounded at the back door. Mom was already in bed, and Aunt Connie was working in her room.

Bob, who had been sitting on the windowsill, made a mad dash for the alcove.

Samantha laughed at his antics. "Some watch cat you are." She stepped into the mud room and peeked out the window before opening the door for Drew.

A leather tool pouch over one shoulder and the red toolbox in hand, he entered. "Evening, Samantha. I guess you know why I'm here."

"Looks like you're planning a major

renovation."

He grinned. "I just need to take some measurements first."

Samantha showed him to the office.

His brow puckered as he surveyed the room.

She crossed her arms. "I'm afraid it's still a disaster area."

"Understandable." He set the toolbox down and removed the pouch from his shoulder.

Feeling out of place, Samantha backed away. "I'll be in the kitchen. Let me know if you need anything."

A few minutes later, Drew passed through on the way out. "I'm going to cut some dowel rods down to size and I'll be right back. Are you okay with Porter coming in?"

Samantha darted a glance toward Bob's hiding place. "Is he cool with the cat?"

Drew nodded. "They're buddies."

She arched a brow. Of course, they were. "No problem, then." She logged onto her laptop and tried to read a few email messages, but Porter's entrance on Drew's heels drove any semblance of concentration from her mind. She was interested to see Bob's behavior when the dog pranced in. He zipped out of hiding to touch noses with Porter and then rubbed against the dog's flank.

Samantha shook her head. "I am amazed."

"They're quite a pair." Drew used the end of one of the trimmed dowel rods to push his cap back. "This won't take long."

Porter reclined near her feet, and Bob curled up next to him.

Samantha scratched behind the dog's ears for a minute, but her interest had followed Drew. She stood carefully so as not to stir the animals. Drawn to the office, she watched while he blocked both windows with the thick dowel rods, cut to fit between the upper frame, which he called the "head," and the sash, or lower window frame.

As he finished the job, she shook her head. "How did you become such an expert on everything?"

He glanced up at her. "Dad was in construction. He was a gifted carpenter who liked to piddle around in the garage in his spare time. He could take junk wood and create amazing things. Furniture, Adirondack chairs, porch swings. Most of our neighbors had something made by him."

"And he taught you?"

He nodded. "I loved hanging with him in his shop."

"Is he still . . . around?" She bit her lip, hoping she hadn't pushed too far. She knew firsthand the pain of losing a parent.

He gave his attention to his tools for a moment. "He passed away when I was overseas."

He'd been overseas. A soldier? "I'm so sorry."

He closed and locked his toolbox. "Thanks. You know how it is." He surveyed the job he'd done. "These windows are secure. Someone would have to remove the entire frame to get in this time."

"Thanks, Drew. We'll all sleep better."

His clear, blue eyes searched hers, but he made no reply.

She forced a smile. "That might be too much to hope for." She turned and led the way back to the kitchen.

On the way out the door, he paused and looked down at her. "Try not to worry about it. This thief seems to know when no one's home."

Cold comfort. The house was too quiet after

Drew and Porter left. She couldn't concentrate on her work, so she headed up to her room. Might as well make it an early night.

Sleep evaded her. She turned over and stared at the ceiling where moonlight's glow shifted through leafy shadows. She could picture someone moving around out there, seeking entry to the darkened downstairs.

At midnight, she was still awake. Her mind raced. Time was short. She only had a few more days. How could she leave Mom alone again knowing someone was trying to get that certificate?

Relax. Deep breath. Don't look at the clock. Pray. Something had to work.

When she woke, daylight brightened the room. Dad's mahogany box was the first thing on her mind. Would she ever see it again?

She glanced at the clock. Six-twenty. Aunt Connie had scheduled a full day that required them to leave the house no later than seven-thirty, which left no time for an energizing run.

Dressed in her favorite blue sun dress, she picked up her purse and hurried downstairs.

When she entered the kitchen, she found Mom

standing in front of the window. Sunshine accented the worry lines in her brow.

Samantha set her purse on the counter. "What is it?"

After a short pause, Mom breathed a soft sigh. "I don't know what to do. After all that has happened, I don't like to leave the house unattended. But I don't want to stay here alone, either."

"I know what you mean. I feel the same way. The certificate is safe, though, isn't it?"

Mom nodded. "Yes, it's in the deposit box. I saw it there last year when I retrieved the insurance policies and Dad's will."

"So, everything should be fine."

Dressed in red slacks with her matching stilettos and a white, cotton jacket, Aunt Connie bustled into the room. Her arms laden with binders, and a large bag looped over one shoulder, she looked from Mom to Samantha. "What should be fine?"

Samantha rushed to help her. "The house— while we're away."

"Where is your faith, ladies?" She handed the stack of binders to Samantha. "Drew should be here any minute. He's going to repair the broken lock on the office window, replace the screen, and install cameras outside."

Mom's mouth dropped open. "What? How did that come about?"

Wasting no time, Aunt Connie opened the back door and stepped outside. "I called him and set it all up last night. This morning, I left a house key in the garage. So, we are good to go."

Mom shook her head and glanced at Samantha. "As usual, your Aunt Connie is ahead of the game."

Before they had finished loading the car, Drew pulled into the drive and parked at the back, near the garage. He lifted a hand in their direction. "Morning, ladies."

Mom looked as though she wanted to visit with him, but Aunt Connie was in a rush. "We have a full day, Eva Grace."

"Yes, boss," Mom said.

Samantha suppressed a giggle as she squeezed into the backseat next to boxes overflowing with donations for swag bags. "Looks like we have our work cut out for us."

Aunt Connie smiled into the rearview mirror.

"Help awaits at the community center."

Samantha had sneaked a quick peek at Aunt Connie's calendar, so she had a rough idea of the day's schedule. After the morning activities, they were headed to Midway, Kentucky, for lunch and then to Mom's preferred dress shop, a small boutique across from the cafe.

Aunt Connie's prediction had been accurate. At least a dozen happy volunteers waited outside the community center, along with a delivery van from *Annie's Cup'o'Brew*.

Aunt Connie winked at Samantha. "Feed them and they will come."

"You are a wonder. How do you manage it? You handled the home situation and organized all of this." Samantha shook her head. "I'm truly inspired."

"I learned from the finest, Samantha, dear. Now I'm doing my best to pass it on to the next generation."

After the long morning of schmoozing and packing swag bags for the gala, Samantha busied herself with answering work emails on her phone while Mom tried on numerous dresses and gowns.

Aunt Connie combed through the racks. "You should look for something too, Samantha. They have some very nice dresses here."

Samantha looked up from her phone. "I have a dress."

"Yes, I've seen it. Your mom wants to buy you a new one. I think you should allow her to. It will mean so much, dear."

Mom handed her final choice to the salesclerk. "My daughter has worn that generic black dress so many times. Help me convince her to at least look at your selection."

Samantha tried to hide behind her phone. They were getting a little too pushy, and she was not fooled—not for one moment. They wanted her to attract a man. Huh! Well, she was not giving in to them this time.

Mom stepped into Samantha's line of vision, holding up a dress.

Samantha's jaw dropped. Satiny, white background shot through with silver threads and glass beads in a swirling pattern, accented with her favorite peacock blue.

Samantha closed her mouth and swallowed. It

wouldn't hurt to try it on.

In the dressing room, she pivoted in front of the mirror. It looked even better than she had imagined. She peeped out the door to where Mom and Aunt Connie waited.

"Does it fit? Do you like it?" Mom asked.

Aunt Connie waved Samantha forward. "Come on out and model it for us."

After one more glance in the mirror, Samantha stepped out.

Mom's eyes shone with moisture.

Aunt Connie clapped her hands. "Oh, Samantha. That dress was made for you."

The salesclerk agreed. "Oh, yes, and it's one-of-a-kind. You will be the only one wearing it."

Samantha bit her lip. Did she dare?

Chapter Ten

A Baseball Story

Samantha rested her head against the back of the car seat as they left Midway. Her eyelids drifted shut, lulled by the peaceful sound of Mom and Aunt Connie's voices. Hard to believe, a few days ago, Mom had bemoaned her sister's visit and wanted nothing more than to stay in bed and be left alone. Maybe Aunt Connie had been right. Mom needed to be needed.

Samantha's anxiety increased whenever she thought about Mom and what would happen when Aunt Connie left. What could Samantha do to help her mother retain the progress she had made?

Move back home.

Where had that thought come from? She shook

her head to dismiss it, but the idea remained. It was impractical. Yes, it was an easy distance and not a bad drive most times, but she'd have to deal with heavy traffic leaving Louisville after work. And sometimes, she was required to work late. An occasional weekend at home might be more feasible. She could attend church with Mom. They could have Sunday dinner together.

Or she could call Mr. Mitchell and see what he had to offer. A job in Shelbyville. Could she go back to living at home full-time?

As the car slowed almost to a stop, Samantha sat forward. What was happening?

Out the passenger-side windows, young foals cavorted in a broad expanse of pasture bounded by double rows of black post-and-rail fencing.

Aunt Connie sighed. "Aren't they gorgeous?"

Mom used her phone to snap a few photos. "This is my favorite time of year, when the youngsters are old enough to mingle and play."

"Shelbyville is the American saddlebred capital of the world," Samantha told her aunt.

Aunt Connie turned to look at Samantha. "So, these are the saddlehorse farms. I read about them when I was researching the area ahead of my trip. Why the double rows of fencing, though? Is it a safety measure?"

Samantha nodded. "Yes. It protects the horses. They can see each other but there's no physical contact. Less chance of fighting. And there's less chance of horses escaping. They might jump the main fence, but there's no room between the two to set up for a second jump."

"Interesting. And why are the fences black? Didn't they all used to be white?" She glanced at Samantha in the mirror.

"I'm not sure why. The black looks better, I think."

Mom took a break from picture-taking to answer, "A few years back, an ordinance was issued that Kentucky equine fences should all be black. It's called equine black and the paint itself tastes bitter, so that discourages the horses from nibbling on the wood."

I had no idea they nibbled on the wood." Aunt Connie eased the car forward at a snail's pace. "Well, I do love driving along these Kentucky back roads with such beautiful scenery and surprises around every bend." She slowed again. "Is that another distillery up ahead?"

"There are a lot of them in this area," Mom said. "That particular distillery is an ancient one. I believe there's an old log cabin up in those trees, where the original owners lived."

They had only driven a few yards when Aunt Connie responded by slowing down again to look for the cabin.

Samantha suppressed an eye roll. Their progress was so slow they might as well be riding in a horse and buggy. Even walking might be faster.

It was late afternoon when they finally reached the outskirts of Shelbyville. A vehicle entering a trailer park caught Samantha's eye. It looked a lot like the car she'd seen parked along the street near Mom's house.

"What kind of car is that?"

Aunt Connie shook her head. "An ugly, brown one."

"Ugh," Mom said. "That's Burke's car."

Samantha perked up. "Who is Burke?"

"Burke Woodford. Your dad's third cousin twice removed, or something like that. He's horrible."

"Have I met him?"

"I doubt it. He only came around a few times. I don't know if you remember that car. It was your grandfather's. Dad was going to sell it after Granddad died but ended up giving it to Burke."

"I don't remember any of this."

"You were away at college. Besides, it wasn't important." She crossed her arms over her chest. "Burke had a way of popping up at the most inopportune times. Not long before he died, Dad was working in the garage and needed something. He told me he was going to the hardware store. He was gone longer than usual, which worried me, so I watched for him. When he got home, that ugly car was following along behind. I hurried upstairs. I did not want to see that man. He always smelled of cigarettes and stale beer, and I couldn't stand to hear him talk."

Aunt Connie had been darting looks at her sister. "Knowing your sweet husband, he was trying to help his cousin."

Mom nodded. "He was, but Burke is the kind of man who will take advantage of a goodhearted person. I'll bet he never worked a day in his life. Well, Jimmy said he served in the Army, so I guess he worked then, but he's been on disability ever since."

Mom could shut down again at any moment. Samantha pressed for more information. "Did Dad let him in the house that day?"

"Of course, he did. That's why I stayed upstairs. I knew what was coming. How many times had I heard that baseball story?" She was quiet for a moment. "What wouldn't I give to hear him tell it again."

Aunt Connie pulled into the driveway. "I wish that, too. Jimmy told the story with such energy and humor."

An ache throbbed in Samantha's chest. How she missed Dad. He had been her hero and constant encourager. "You can do anything you set your mind to," he loved to say. "Don't be afraid to dream big, Sammie love."

She had to get that baseball back.

She carried the two dress bags into the house and hung them on the coat rack in the mudroom. Her mind reeled with this new information. Dad had welcomed his cousin, Burke, into their home and shown him the mahogany box and its contents. He'd told the story, so she would bet he also bragged of its worth. Had he mentioned the certificate?

A soft, intermittent beeping noise drew Samantha into the hall. The sound was coming from the office. Must've been the new system Drew had installed. Would it always beep like that? Annoying.

The door stood open. Its usual musty smell had been replaced with the odor of fresh wood and paint. A sticky note on the desktop gave instructions for logging into the camera program.

Aunt Connie joined Samantha.

Mom hung back, still refusing to enter the room.

Samantha shrugged. "Well, it's a mess, of course, but looks like Drew did a good job on the windows. He left instructions on the security cameras."

Aunt Connie checked her phone. "I let him know we're home, so he can stop by anytime."

Mom sighed. "I'm exhausted. Can we just heat up a can of soup or something for dinner?"

Samantha crossed the room to give her mom a

sideways hug. "I'll take care of it. Why don't you change into your comfortable clothes and relax?"

After Mom headed upstairs, Samantha checked her phone. "Oh, and the insurance agent will be here in a few minutes. Looks like we'll have a busy evening."

"Let's order pizza," Aunt Connie said. "Then you won't have to worry about it and cleanup will be easy."

Samantha agreed. "I like that idea." She headed to the kitchen to find the number.

"Get enough to share in case Drew comes by. He said if he had time, he'd stop in and give us a quick tutorial on this thing."

Samantha sighed. After placing the order, she settled onto a stool and rested her head in her hands. She needed time to process everything that had happened. Burke's car was recognizable. She could drive through the trailer park and find where he lived.

She bit her lip. What if she found him? What would she do then, confront him? Knock on his door and ask if he broke into their home and stole Dad's mahogany box?

Probably not a good idea. However, the more Samantha thought about it, the more she wanted to know where that man lived. She could stake it out, maybe come up with some helpful clue.

She lifted her head at the sound of Aunt Connie's footsteps in the hall.

"Drew won't be coming, but he told me how to shut off the beeping noise. He said it was most likely a spider or something like that. He'll be by sometime tomorrow to tweak the settings."

Samantha got up and moved a few dirty dishes from the sink to the dishwasher. She should be relieved that Drew wasn't coming. Instead, she felt disappointment. Weird.

Aunt Connie was still talking. "Eva Grace will not step foot in that room. Do you think she'd consider re-purposing it?"

Samantha turned to look at her. "As what?"

"A downstairs guest room, or a craft room? You could hire someone to help move that heavy desk upstairs. Didn't your dad used to talk about moving his office up there?"

"He did. It's a good idea. I'm not sure Mom will go for it."

Aunt Connie patted her shoulder. "We should at least try. It could make a real difference."

"I guess. We have to clean it up, anyway. I'll think about it. Also, I was wondering what the schedule is for tomorrow?"

"Briarbeck's Stables in the morning. Nancy has invited us to stay for lunch afterward."

"Mind if I drive separately? I need to stop by the grocery on the way home."

Chapter Eleven

Horses to Trailers

Tantalizing smells emanated from the kitchen when Samantha returned from her early morning run. Blueberries?

Bob rubbed his big, yellow head against her ankle and purred as Samantha slipped out of her running shoes. She bent and picked him up. "What's going on, boy? Who is baking, huh?" After a quick peek around the corner, she drew back, mouth agape.

Mom hadn't seen her, so Samantha backed away, not wanting to spoil the surprise. If it was a surprise. It was most unexpected. She set Bob down and then tiptoed upstairs for a quick shower.

Jeans and a pink scooped-necked tee seemed

appropriate riding attire. Samantha dug around in her closet until she found a pair of long-abandoned boots, so she needn't worry about stable hazards.

By the time she descended the stairs again, Mom and Aunt Connie were preparing to leave.

"You look like a cowgirl." Aunt Connie winked and smiled. "Too bad you missed breakfast. Your mom made blueberry muffins." She held up a plastic container filled with muffins.

Muffins meant for someone else.

Mom planted a kiss on Samantha's cheek. "Good morning, sweetheart. I left you a muffin and the coffee's still hot, I think." She tucked her purse beneath her arm and picked up a tray of homemade cookies.

Samantha smiled. "Those look delicious."

Mom moved the plate away. "These are for the children, but I kept a few for us to enjoy later."

"Great." Samantha held the door open for them. "I'll be there soon."

Her phone vibrated. She'd forgotten to turn the sound back on. The call went straight to voice mail.

Mom had not lost her gift for baking. Samantha chewed a blueberry-laden bite as she filled a to-go cup with coffee and then headed out the door.

In the car, she clicked on the most recent voice mail message.

"Tuttle here. I just wanted to keep you updated. No luck on the prints. We'll keep working on it."

Hmm. *They'll keep working on it.* She sipped coffee and finished her muffin as she drove to the Briarbeck Farm, enjoying the chance to be on her own again. Though she looked forward to seeing Miss Nancy and possibly having a chance to ride one of the horses, her mind kept skipping over those pleasantries.

Last night, she had made a plan for the afternoon—a plan her mother would not approve—a trip to that trailer park on the south side of town.

She hadn't lied to Aunt Connie. She did plan to stop at the grocery at some point.

What did she expect to find? The mahogany box on display outside the man's trailer? No, but maybe a clue, or some indication of his innocence. She could be wrong in suspecting him. He may not be the uncouth character her mom had described. Mom could be a little harsh in her judgments.

She popped the last bite of muffin into her

mouth and chewed. She was tired of waiting, tired of feeling helpless. Taking a look around that trailer park might be foolish, but it would be forward motion.

By the time she arrived at the farm, everyone was milling around the stable area waiting for the children's arrival. Except for Aunt Connie, of course, who sat on the Briarbeck's veranda, talking on the phone.

Mom arranged the muffins and cookies on a table beneath a pop-up canopy. "Samantha, Nancy was just looking for you. I think she's in her office."

On the way to Nancy's office, Samantha paused to greet one of the few horses still in the stables, a gelding. The animal nuzzled her hair and nickered.

"Samantha, is that you?" Dressed in jeans and wearing her signature blue cowboy boots, Nancy closed the distance between them to give Samantha a hug. "Perfect timing, girl. I was just about to tack up your favorite horse." She gestured toward the gelding.

Nancy's blond hair had lightened, and her slender face held more crinkles than when Samantha had last seen her. "Grady the Grump?"

"Grady is a grump no more. Mellowed out over the years, like me." She grinned as she slipped the bridle over Grady's head and then opened the stable door. "I hope you've kept up with your riding."

"No. I haven't made time for it."

"Well, you should. I'm opening back up, so I expect to see you here." She put her arm around Samantha's shoulders. "Often."

"I will. I mean, I would love that." And it would give her another excuse to come home on the weekends.

They walked out of the stables as the van pulled up the drive.

Nancy beamed as she handed Grady's reins to one of her stable hands. "I am so over-the-top excited about today."

Samantha had to laugh. "I can see that."

Within minutes, a dozen kids perched on hay bales in rapt attention as Nancy gave her classic first lesson in riding. The children repeated her riding rules with enthusiasm.

Mom stepped beside Samantha. "Brings back memories, doesn't it? Seems like yesterday." She patted Samantha's arm.

Seeing her mom so upbeat sent a wave of warmth through Samantha. "Yes, it does. How I loved those days."

While Nancy and her crew worked to get the first group of children seated on their mounts, Samantha was drawn to a familiar face.

Carson, the little boy that Porter had singled out at the picnic, made his way to a placid, brown mare.

Samantha rushed to help him, but there was no need. He did fine on his own.

Balanced on his crutches, he reached out and touched the mare's nose and then leaned his forehead against her neck.

Samantha dropped into a crouch beside him. "Do you know this horse?"

He shook his head. "No, but Mr. Drew told me not to be afraid. He said Miss Nancy would give me a gentle one."

"Well, he was right." She rose, intending to help him up, but hesitated because of the boy's leg braces. Would the animal shy away from the metal?

Nancy joined them. "I chose Lady Gwendolyn because she has worked with braces before. She just needs to see them." With a nod toward Samantha, she beckoned for Carson to move off to the side a little, so the mare could get a good look at him.

Carson laughed when Lady Gwendolyn tossed her head and whinnied.

Nancy and Samantha lifted the boy into the saddle. Once they had him strapped in, Nancy led the horse forward. "Samantha, we could use your help as a side-walker."

Samantha stepped alongside as Nancy led Lady Gwendolyn and her precious mount into the circle of riders. Each horse had a lead and two side-walkers. "Are these all volunteers?"

Nancy cast a glance over her shoulder. "Four of them are from Home of the Innocents, but the rest are my volunteers. I have the most wonderful friends."

After their rides, the children visited the refreshment table and carried their snacks to the hay bale circle.

Samantha walked with Carson as he returned to the bus. His excited chatter warmed her heart. When all the children were in their seats, the driver pulled away.

Nancy's phone rang. "Thank you. We're on our

way."

Samantha, Mom, and Aunt Connie followed Nancy to the veranda that spanned the back of the house.

Nancy held one of the French doors open for them to enter. "The food is inside. After we fill our plates, we'll meet back out here."

Aunt Connie hooked arms with Samantha. "Al fresco dining with a pastoral view. I love it."

Just inside the door, an antique sideboard held an array of fruits and cheeses, small sandwiches, a tossed salad, and a plate of chocolate chip cookies. A bowl of roses and Stargazer lilies scented the air.

While Mom and Nancy entertained Aunt Connie with stories of Briarbeck's former days, Samantha struggled to give them her full attention. Her mind was filled with Burke, the brown car, and the trailer park—if only she could swat those thoughts and send them flying away until it was time to go.

Mom shook her head and sighed. "Those were the glory days, weren't they?"

Nancy responded by raising her glass. "To the glory days ahead of us."

After drinking to the toast, Aunt Connie pushed away from the table. "I hate to break up this wonderful respite, but I have a to-do list a mile long. I hope you're planning to attend the gala."

Nancy led the way to the front drive. "Oh, yes. I am so excited about it. I know it's going to be the event of the year."

Samantha lingered long enough to help Nancy clean up. She did not want Mom and Aunt Connie to see the direction she took.

A few minutes later, driving at a snail's pace through the narrow streets of the trailer park, she watched for a familiar, coppery-brown sedan.

Most of the trailers looked clean and their yards well-tended. A few residents sat outside or paused in their yard work to watch with obvious curiosity as she passed.

At the end of one long street, she spied the car parked in front of an ancient, blue and white trailer. The yard was not well kept like the others. Tufts of grass grew here and there in the weed-filled lawn and an overflowing garbage can sat near the curb.

Two small containers with a familiar emblem caught her eye. They looked like the ones she had found on Dad's desk. After a quick look around, she put the car in park and grabbed her phone.

On the pretense of checking the rear tire, she snapped a couple of up-close photos of the containers. Among the beer cans and fast-food wrappers, a white, plastic bag ruffled in the breeze. She couldn't see the name on the bag. She tugged at it, setting off a frenzy of buzzing flies and releasing an odor almost as bad as what she'd found in the office. She wrinkled her nose and continued to tug until the bag fell off the heap onto the ground where she could read the label.

Mac's Deli. She snapped another photo.

"What do you think you're doing?"

Chapter Twelve

Cousin's Cuisine

The gruff voice prickled Samantha's scalp. She tucked the phone into her jeans pocket and rose. The man in the trailer's doorway looked to be about five-ten with a paunch that hung over his belt. He wore wrinkled jeans and a too-small white tee shirt. A chunk of salt-and-pepper hair hung over one eye.

Could this scowling man be related to her father? "I . . . I thought I had a flat tire. It isn't . . . um, flat. I guess I just ran over . . . something."

She inched backward, planning to dash around the car to the driver's side and jump in. Until her curiosity piqued. She glanced at the copper-brown Buick. "Are you Burke?"

He stepped out onto a porch that swayed with

his weight. His scowl darkened. "Who's asking?"

"Um, Samantha Carr."

Recognition did nothing to ease the frown on his ruddy face. "Are you here to take back the car, too?"

What? She shook her head. "N . . . no, I'm not. I recognized it as my granddad's, that's all. I . . . I remembered Dad gave it to a family member, a . . . a cousin of his, I think." She shook her head. "I don't want it. No."

He waved her away. "Scram, then. Get on out of here. I want nothing to do with you or any of your lying family."

Samantha stared back at him. Lying? Who lied? "I'm sorry, I didn't mean to—"

"You heard me. Get on out of here!"

The window curtains across the street parted as someone looked out to see what the commotion was.

Bristling against Burke's false accusation, Samantha forced her feet into motion. She opened the door, got in, and took off.

What a creep. He was everything her mother said and more.

Her hands shook and her heart thumped like

crazy as she wove through the streets back to the entrance. As her pulse rate slowed, her ire dimmed. She replayed their conversation.

What had he meant? Who had lied to him, and why did he ask if she had come to take back the car?

Her mother was humming when Samantha entered the kitchen and set two grocery bags on the counter.

Drying her hands on an apron, Mom faced Samantha. "There you are. I hope you remembered the ranch dressing. We're all out."

"I did."

"Drew is coming for dinner. He's going to show us how to work the alarm system."

Samantha paused to sniff the air. "Is that roast chicken?"

"Yes, it is." She paused before putting the groceries away. "Why don't you get some rest. You look tired."

Not tired. Still in shock. Though she would

rather stay busy and not think about her encounter with Burke, Samantha took her mother's suggestion and headed upstairs.

In her room, she sat on her bed and tried to concentrate on email messages, but her heart wasn't in it. She sank back against her pillows and closed her eyes. The worst part was, she couldn't talk to anyone about the episode. What had happened that day when Burke visited Dad? Perhaps Dad offended him in some way.

When her phone pinged, Samantha found several text messages she hadn't noticed earlier. Her boss had needed an answer to a question she'd sent via email yesterday.

Yesterday. She grimaced. Not good.

The email requested information on a well-known Louisville gift shop. She spent the next hour researching the shop to see what had been done in the past, marketing-wise. She was attaching the completed report to an email when the doorbell rang.

A moment later, she heard Drew's voice downstairs and a moment after that, her phone pinged again. This time, it was Mom letting her know dinner was ready.

Samantha chuckled. Before smartphones, Mom had stood at the base of the stairs and called her name. *Samantha, dinner!* Or, *Samantha, telephone!*

She had to admit, texting was quieter. More civilized.

Porter thumped his tail but didn't get up as Samantha entered the kitchen. Probably didn't want to disturb Bob, who was curled up next to him. Samantha bent to pet both.

From across the room, Drew greeted her with a smile and then turned back to Aunt Connie. "I'm happy to help out with that. I can round up a couple of guys. Let me know when you want it done."

Aunt Connie was pouring tea into glasses. She handed one to Drew. "That sounds great, thanks."

Samantha crossed to the island sink and washed her hands. She looked from Drew to Aunt Connie. "Help with what?"

Mom set a massive bowl of salad in the middle of the table. "We're moving the office into the attic space."

Samantha turned to look at her. "Who are you, and what have you done with my mom?"

Mom laughed out loud.

Aunt Connie's eyes sparkled as she poured another glass of tea and passed it to Samantha.

Glass in hand, Samantha crossed to the table. "Have you decided what you want to do with that room?"

"I have always wanted a craft room. Your father almost talked me into turning your room into something like that, but I'm glad we put it off."

"So am I." Samantha set her glass down so she could take the platter of sliced chicken from her mother and place it on the table. What a lot of food. She eyed her mom. Funny how she was so animated when Drew was around.

What would happen when everyone went home? How would Mom react when left on her own again?

Samantha took a deep breath and exhaled.

She hadn't noticed Drew's approach until she heard his voice behind her. "Are you all right?" He pulled out a chair for her. His eyes shone with genuine concern.

With a slow nod, she sank into the chair. "Yes, thank you, I'm fine." At least, she would be.

After dinner, Aunt Connie loaded the dishwasher while Drew instructed Samantha and Mom on the alarm system.

"This is one of the most user-friendly systems available," he told Mom. "Still, if you run into any problems, just shoot me a text."

Mom blew out a breath. "You know I'm not computer savvy. I'm going to need written directions."

When Samantha's phone vibrated, she glanced at the display. Her boss again. She made eye contact with Mom. "Sorry, I need to take this call." On the way to the Florida room, she pressed the redial.

"Samantha, I'm sorry to bother you so late. I wanted to make sure you had received my messages. This job is important, and we're in a time crunch."

"Yes, ma'am, I apologize. We were out most of the day. I sent the information you requested. You should have it in your email."

She responded with a relieved sigh. "Thank you. You're the best. I also wanted to let you know I received the invitation to your aunt's gala. Thank you so much for including me. As much as I would love to participate in anything associated with the

Wright Foundation, we have another event that evening and won't be able to attend. Please thank your aunt for me. I would like to send a donation. Will you be in town anytime soon, or shall I mail it?"

"I need to go to the craft store, so I can pick it up in the morning if you like."

"Great, and again, please give Miss Wright my best wishes."

The thought of a donation from her boss pricked Samantha's conscience. She massaged her temples. Would she be obligated to stay at her job?

Mom, Drew, and Aunt Connie were still in the kitchen, engaged in lively conversation. Longing for a moment alone, Samantha wandered out the side door.

Sunset painted the western sky with swaths of peach and apricot. A soft breeze picked up the scent of Mom's wild roses entwined around an arbor beside the garage. With a sigh, Samantha sank to the steps and took it all in. How she had missed this.

Like the tendrils of the invasive Chinese privet so prevalent in the area, Samantha's troubled thoughts found their way back into her mind. Why was Burke so angry? Who had lied to him? Certainly not Dad. He had always insisted on honesty and forthrightness.

Porter rounded the side of the house, took one look at her, and decided she needed his help. He plopped down beside her and gave a soft whine.

She bent to pet him. "You're right this time, buddy." She rubbed his chin. "I could use a good listener right now."

The door opened, and Drew stepped out. "He's the best. Trustworthy and nonjudgmental."

Samantha buried her face in Porter's neck and muttered between her teeth, "And his master has impeccable timing."

He stepped past her to the ground. "Care to go for a stroll? Porter needs a walk before I take off." He attached a leash to the dog's collar.

Samantha hesitated and then rose to join him. She could confide in Drew. As a counselor, he was bound to discretion.

Once they were away from the house, she gave him a brief description of her visit to the trailer park. "I suppose it was foolish of me. But I hadn't expected to run into him."

"You said you saw the same containers you found in the office?"

She retrieved her phone from the back pocket of her jeans and found the photo. "It's from Mac's Deli, I think."

He examined the photo. "That's a popular place. It's in a gas station on LaGrange Road, not far from that trailer community." He scrolled to the next photo. "And this is?"

"A bag from the deli, I guess. I sort of dislodged it from the trash can."

His brow furrowed. "Trash piled up like that suggests he's late on his refuse bill. Lots of weeds in the lawn, too."

"Yeah, his place is pretty rundown."

He handed her phone back. "Next time your curiosity kicks up, give me a call. I'd rather you didn't take chances. Sounds like there might be bad blood between him and your branch of the family."

"I don't know why there would be. Dad tried to help him. He even gave him a car that had belonged to my grandfather." She glanced at the photo again and was about to swipe it closed when something caught her eye. She stopped walking. "Wait." She clicked on it and enlarged the photo. "Wait— that's—that looks like . . ." She looked at Drew.

"What is it?"

She turned her phone screen toward him. "I recognize that green ribbon. It looks like the bundle of envelopes that Dad kept in the mahogany box. It's wedged beneath the garbage can."

The Visitor Has a Ball

Chapter Thirteen

To the Letter

"This could be proof he took the box." Samantha covered her mouth as understanding dawned.

Drew closed the space between them and looked over her shoulder.

She glanced up at him. Gosh, he smelled good. "Burke is the burglar."

He stepped back. "The picture is kind of blurred. How can you be certain that's a bundle of envelopes?"

She reduced the photo with her fingertips. "I have to check it out. If it is what I think it is, maybe Detective Tuttle will question Burke."

Drew still looked doubtful. "Burke could say

you planted those when you were there earlier."

She hadn't thought of that. "Still, I want those letters. Those were written by my great-grandfather." She pocketed her phone and started toward home. "I need to go back there."

Drew caught up to her. "Now, hold on. You can't do that. If he sees you, there could be trouble. I'll go."

"But it'll be dark soon. I know the exact location."

"Then you can go with me, but you have to stay in the truck. I'll park well away from his trailer and act like I'm walking Porter."

She chewed her lip. It was a good idea.

"I drive a landscaping truck. No one will question why I'm in the area. I could duck down in front of that can like I'm cleaning up after my dog and grab the . . . whatever that is. Assuming it's still there."

"It will be." Hope brought a smile to her lips as she walked. The thing was, what would Mom say when she left with Drew? Her steps faltered near the back door. "What will we tell Mom? And Aunt Connie? Where should we say we're going?"

Drew shrugged. "A guy and a girl going for a drive. Is that so strange?"

Samantha bit her lip as she thought it through. Not strange, no. Exactly what Mom and Aunt Connie would love to see, but she couldn't tell Drew about that. She pulled in a deep breath and stepped through the back door into the kitchen. "Drew and I are going out for a little while."

The sisters exchanged glances.

Samantha kept a calm countenance. "It's just a drive."

Mom looked up. "Of course, it is. Why would we think otherwise?"

Drew stepped inside. "And possibly ice cream. Can we bring you anything?"

Aunt Connie shook her head. "No, thank you. I have an early morning, so I'll be turning in soon."

With a definite twinkle in her eyes, Mom waved her hand. "You two go on and have fun."

Samantha could imagine the course of the conversation as soon as they left. She hated to dash her mother's hopes, but she had no intention of starting a romance.

Drew held the truck's door open for her.

She climbed in next to Porter and fastened her seatbelt.

Porter snuggled into her lap.

She could do worse than Drew Lindner and Porter Wagger. She had done worse, but that was all behind her now. She would not make that mistake again.

Drew backed out of the driveway. "I was thinking, say this Burke guy was involved and you're able to get Tuttle to check it out. There's no guarantee Burke still has the baseball. He may have already sold it."

"I know. But at least we'll know what happened to it. I'd rather have the box back, if he still has it, and those letters."

"You said your great-grandfather wrote the letters?"

She nodded. "He wrote them to my great-grandmother, Tildy, while he was in Europe. He fought in World War II."

"I take it you've read these letters?"

She ran her fingers through Porter's silky coat. "Many times. They were wonderful. He was a very intelligent man. After he returned home, he started the accounting company that Dad eventually took over. A company that supported three generations of the Carr family."

"But not you? You didn't have an interest in the family business?"

She shook her head. "Not at all, so Dad sold it to his partners before he retired. I was relieved to see it go. I am not a numbers person. Not like he was."

Drew nodded his understanding as he drove through the main entrance into the trailer park. "Where do I go from here?"

Samantha's stomach clenched as she directed him. "It's near the end of the street on the right. It's the unkempt one—hard to miss."

Drew found a vacant lot and parked in front of it. He reached over the back of the seat, grabbed his cap, and put it on. Then he opened the door and stepped out. "Would you mind handing me Porter's leash? It's in the glove compartment. Oh, and a couple of those little bags."

Samantha passed him the leash and two of the bags.

He eyed her as he fastened the leash to Porter's collar. "Remember, stay in the truck." He tucked the bags in his pants pocket and backed away.

She sat back and folded her hands in her lap. "Yes, sir."

Before jumping out, Porter's steady gaze held hers.

Samantha huffed out a sigh. "I will. I promise."

With a dazzling smile that took Samantha's breath, Drew closed the door. "Let's go, boy."

If only she had thought to dig out her old night vision goggles. She hadn't seen them since sixth grade, but knowing Mom, they were still around. She'd bet they were in the attic.

Samantha kept her attention on that tall guy striding up the street, stopping for Porter to do what dogs do on walks. The man's patience astounded her at times.

Then he halted and knelt. After several very long minutes, he stood and started back.

Had he found it? Was it Great-grandfather Carr's packet of letters? Her breath caught in her throat as he approached.

No eye contact. Huh.

He removed Porter's leash before opening the door.

Porter hopped up and settled beside Samantha.

Drew removed his cap before holding the bag in front of her. "Pay dirt."

She reached for it.

He pulled it away. "Don't remove the letters. I didn't touch them. Maybe there will be fingerprints."

Tears stung her eyes as she accepted the plastic bag. She tightened her grip, feeling the shape of the envelopes beneath her fingertips. "Thank you, Drew."

He got in and closed the door. "You don't know how hard it was for me to see such a scandalous lawn."

Samantha laughed. "I did warn you."

"Yes, you did." Leaning forward, he opened the glove compartment and returned the leash and the unused plastic bag. As he did, he peered at her. "If you like, I can drop those by the police department in the morning."

She nodded. "Okay. Maybe it would be better coming from you."

"Now, how about that ice cream?"

Samantha answered with a smile. A weight had

lifted off her shoulders.

By ten after nine, they sat at an outside table in front of the Dairy Freeze with a big, yellow moon as a backdrop.

Porter reclined at their feet.

Samantha couldn't help admiring such an obedient animal. Most dogs she'd been around begged at the table.

Drew spooned in a bite of double chocolate ice cream. "Are you enjoying the time away from that high-stress job?"

Samantha smiled at Mom's usual description of her occupation. "More than I expected." She stirred the strawberry topping into her scoop of vanilla ice cream before taking a bite. "I hadn't realized how much I missed our little town."

He shook his head. "Not so little anymore."

"True. Compared to Louisville, though, it is." She took another bite. "I'm thinking of spending more time here."

"Your mom will like that."

She watched his expression. Had Mom complained to him? "I feel a little guilty for abandoning Mom, even though she encouraged me to."

"She wanted you to have your independence."

"Yes. I'm just not sure she was ready to be alone. And the house . . . without Dad . . ." She bowed her head.

He hesitated before answering. "You lost someone, too." He sat back. "I can't go into detail, of course, but she is recovering. It's been a slow process."

"Thanks for your help."

"It's what I do."

"You seem good at it, especially with children."

"Well, Porter and I are a team. I have to give him most of the credit."

She propped an elbow on the table and leaned her chin on the palm of her hand. "How did you become interested in working with a therapy dog?"

He pushed his empty ice cream container away. "It's kind of a long story."

"And I'm prying."

He smiled and shook his head. "No, it's not that. It's time to get you home, Miss Carr."

Samantha stood and walked with him to the truck. She waited in silence as he stepped around to the driver's side and climbed in. Would he answer her question?

Drew started the engine and pulled out of the parking lot. When he stopped at a traffic light, he began to speak. "Five years ago, I . . . was injured in Afghanistan. It was my second tour. I recovered from the physical injuries, but then I was diagnosed with PTSD. After my discharge, I came back home. I thought if I was near family, and I got back into church, I could recover on my own." After a long pause, he continued. "I did improve, but not well enough. A friend of my sister's suggested therapy dogs. My sister did the research and found an excellent program based in Michigan. She drove me there with the hope that I could find a good match."

He parked along the street in front of the house. "It was there that Porter found me. The bond was instant. I decided to stay for a while and learn as much as I could. Maybe I could help others in the same situation. After two years, I came back here to get my degree." He opened the door and got out. "Stay, Porter."

Though she was capable of opening her own door and climbing out of the truck, Samantha waited for Drew.

Porter nuzzled her ear.

She scratched his chin. "See ya later, buddy."

Drew walked all the way to the front door with her and waited as she unlocked it.

She turned to look at him. "Thanks for . . . everything." She held out her hand.

He gave her hand a light squeeze before releasing it. "Anytime. I'll let you know when I've dropped off the envelopes."

She nodded her thanks and stepped inside. After closing the door, she moved to the window and watched as Drew returned to his vehicle and drove away. Her determination to remain aloof ebbed away with the sound of the truck's engine.

The Visitor Has a Ball

Chapter Fourteen

Alarming Episode

"Ping-ping-ping."

Samantha didn't want to wake up. It was too soon.

Ping-ping-ping.

Weird. What was that?

"Samantha!"

Mom?

Aunt Connie opened the door and leaned in. "Samantha, the alarm. Someone's out there."

Samantha sat up and blinked her eyes. With a quick glance at the clock, she threw back the covers. "It's two-thirty in the morning."

"Yes, it is," Aunt Connie called from the stairs.

In the kitchen, Mom and Aunt Connie hovered

over the tablet Drew had set up for the cameras.

"There," Aunt Connie directed. "Click on that one."

Mom touched the screen and then sucked in a breath. "Someone was out there."

Aunt Connie nodded. "I told you so. I heard a banging noise and then a car engine roared. I think the alarm must have scared him off."

Samantha peered at the screen. "Check some of the other cameras. Maybe there's one that caught the car driving away."

Mom checked the camera footage, but it was too dark. The red cast of brake lights in front of the house was all they could make out.

The doorbell rang, followed by someone banging on the door. All three of them jumped.

Aunt Connie took the lead. "That will be the police. You two stay here. I'm the only one wearing a robe."

Samantha looked down at her oversized tee and folded her arms over her chest. What if the officers needed to see the camera footage? She ran upstairs, grabbed Mom's robe and one for herself, just in case. Aunt Connie had returned to the kitchen by the time Samantha made it back downstairs.

Aunt Connie looked up when Samantha walked in. "They're checking outside. I told them we have camera footage. Do you know how to forward it to them? Here's the info." She held a bright, pink sticky note between her fingers.

When Samantha reached for it, Mom touched her arm. "Show me, so I can do it when you're not here."

Samantha pulled in a breath and released it. "I hope you won't ever have to, Mom. But sure, I'll show you how."

Samantha led Mom through the steps, jotting them down on a notepad as they went along. "Now, you just attach the file to an email and send it."

Mom clicked send and then sat back. "Well, you're right. It was easy." She ran her finger down the list on the paper. "I should be able to figure this out."

Almost a half-hour later, Aunt Connie answered a knock at the door.

Samantha waited near the stairs. She hoped to hear their conversation, but it was too muffled.

Aunt Connie closed the door and returned to the

kitchen. "They've gone. They think the thief was spooked by the alarm and probably won't return. I told them we sent the video."

Fighting emotions, Samantha nodded. "Mom has the instructions if she needs them." She bit her lip.

Aunt Connie pulled her into a hug. "It will be all right. They will find this guy." She stepped back. "Now, we should all go back to bed and try to get some rest. I checked all the locks."

Mom stood. "And I reset the alarm. Not sure if I can go back to sleep, though."

Samantha swiped her palms over her cheeks. "Let's put on an old movie. I'll watch with you."

Aunt Connie patted her shoulder, "Thank you. I'm going to bed." She hugged Mom. "I hope you can get some rest. You and I have that trip to Floyds Knobs in the morning to visit Paul."

In her bedroom, Mom fluffed her pillows and turned on the television. She found *The Magic of Ordinary Days* and started it.

As the familiar theme song played, Samantha snuggled close to her. "My favorite."

Mom kissed her forehead. "I know. I recorded

it the last time it played."

Bob jumped on the bed and curled up on Mom's lap.

It wasn't long before Mom's eyelids drooped and her even breathing assured Samantha that she slept.

Samantha stayed a while longer, trying to stave off the inevitable anger. That man! He was not going to give up. Something had to be done about him.

Samantha entered the kitchen at half past seven and headed straight for the coffee pot.

Aunt Connie looked up from her laptop. "Good morning. I was just wondering about the plans for the booth. Do you need to shop for supplies?"

"I thought I could do that while you and Mom are at Uncle Paul's." After filling her cup, she slid the pot back on the warmer as a memory surfaced. "Oh, my goodness. With all that's happened, I forgot to tell you. Though my boss declined your invitation to the gala, she's making a donation. I told her I would stop in at the office and pick it up this morning."

"Wonderful. Take her one of the swag bags. Do you remember where we put them?"

Samantha nodded. "I do. She'll love that. Then I'll go by the craft store while I'm in Louisville."

Aunt Connie nodded. "Sounds like a good plan. Show me what you've got in mind for the booth."

She sat next to Aunt Connie at the breakfast bar, opened her phone, and pulled up the list of supplies she'd created. "I thought a fake window backdrop would be cute with intertwining vines and flowers. There's an old window frame in the garage, and Mom has some lace curtains in the attic."

"Great idea. Goes right along with the garden theme. You should be able to set it all up or at least get started on it tomorrow. Do you think you can get Drew to help you?"

Samantha shrugged. "Maybe. He'll be here with Mom. I'm sure we can at least depend on him to deliver the window frame."

"Great. I'll leave it in your capable hands." She closed her laptop, stood, and gathered her dishes. After placing them in the dishwasher, she dried her hands, picked up her computer, and kissed Samantha's cheek. "If I don't see you before we leave, drive safely." She tapped her finger on the table in front of Samantha. "Don't forget. We're having dinner with Nancy Briarbeck and a few of her friends tonight. Six o'clock."

Samantha sat back. "Did I know about that?"

"Have you checked your email this morning?"

Uh, no. "I will do that right now. Give Uncle Paul a hug for me." Samantha checked her email and added *Six o'clock dinner at Nancy's* to her calendar. Then she read through the supply list again, but her mind kept returning to last night's attempted break-in.

This morning, Drew would deliver the packet of letters to Detective Tuttle. She considered sending Tuttle a text to give him a head's up, but would that defeat the purpose of sending Drew? Maybe it was best if she stayed out of it.

Samantha blew out an exasperated breath as she

endured late afternoon traffic in Louisville. Stopping in at the office had been a bad idea. Someone had misplaced a file. Samantha found it and that led to another thing and then another. It was after four when she left. No time to stop at the craft store.

A lane shutdown on I-64 added to the usual evening snarl of traffic. She pulled into Mom's driveway with only a few minutes to spare.

Half an hour later, she got into the Lexus for the short trip to Nancy's. On the way, Mom and Aunt Connie talked about their lovely day in Floyds Knobs.

Aunt Connie glanced at Samantha in the rearview mirror. "The knobs are so beautiful. Uncle Paul took us on a lovely drive after lunch. Some of the houses overlooking the golf course—oh my." She pulled into the lane at Briarbeck's and found a parking spot near several other vehicles.

Samantha suppressed a sigh. It was going to be a long evening.

Dinner was a blur. Missing sleep the night before had taken its toll. She did her best to smile and be personable, but it couldn't end soon enough.

She crawled into bed at a quarter after ten and fell into an exhausted sleep.

Bleary-eyed, Samantha turned off her alarm. Six-thirty. Thursday morning. How had it been a week already? She ran three miles, showered, and entered the kitchen before eight-thirty. Not bad. A sticky note on the coffee pot read, *Early meeting with staff at venue. See you later—Aunt Connie.*

She carried her cup to the Florida room and stood for a moment, gazing at the back garden. It was a vision of loveliness, thanks to Drew. Pushing aside thoughts of the man and his dog, she sank into a chair and opened her Bible app to 1 Kings 19. She read the passage from Sunday's sermon again. What was God trying to tell her through this?

Trust.

She set her phone down. That was a tough one. Wasn't it what she was asking of her mother?

A noise in the kitchen alerted her to Mom's presence and the lateness of the hour.

"Is that you, Samantha?"

"Good morning." She kissed Mom's cheek and gave her a sideways hug. "I'm headed to the craft store. I hope you have a restful day."

"I hope so, too, after all that's happened this week. You be careful out there. The road construction makes driving hazardous."

Samantha arrived at the craft store shortly after they opened. She swept through the aisles, collected what she needed, and checked out. No time for browsing today. On the way back, she made a quick stop at the outlet mall to pick up a treat for Mom.

Instead of getting on the interstate, she took a back road that would lead past the trailer park. What could it hurt to drive by?

Burke would have no trouble recognizing her little red car, so she left it in the empty lot where Drew had parked last night and proceeded on foot.

As she approached Burke's trailer, her steps slowed. The old car was parked sideways across the drive. It looked as though he had driven over his garbage can. Trash littered the street in front of the trailer.

Samantha wrinkled her nose at the smell as she picked her way around the car to the front porch. She put one hand on the trailer's outer wall to balance herself as she stepped up on the rickety structure.

There was no sound coming from inside the

trailer. Maybe he was still sleeping. Her hand poised to knock, she drew back as the inner door swung open with such violence, the porch shook.

Burke pushed the storm door open a couple of inches. "What d'you want?"

She grimaced as she took in his appearance. The island-style shirt he wore was stained and wrinkled. His hair stuck straight up in front, as though he had been sleeping on his face, which was contorted in anger. Samantha had only ever seen angry reactions from Burke. He was a pitiful mess of a man.

She swallowed. "I have a question for you. Did you take my dad's box?"

His eyes bulged and lips convulsed. "You got your nerve! Get outta here before I call the cops!"

Samantha's pulse quickened, throbbing in her throat. She crossed her arms over her chest. "You go right ahead and call them. I'll wait."

Still sputtering hateful words, he slammed the door, which sent a tremor through the trailer.

Samantha half expected the whole thing to collapse. Sensing someone watching, she turned. Three women and an elderly man stood in the neighbor's yard. One of the women, dressed in shorts, a University of Kentucky tee shirt, and flip flops, waved to her.

Samantha left the porch and stepped toward the group.

"We've called the police," the woman said. "They're on the way."

Oh no. Samantha shook her head. "I'm sorry. I didn't mean to cause trouble."

The woman huffed. "Oh, you didn't, hon. We called them before you got here. That idiot has been raving all morning." She pointed to the street. "Look what he did in the wee hours. Took out two of our mailboxes and ruined my roses. Not to mention that horrible stink from his nasty trash can. He's a menace to the neighborhood."

The old man nodded. "We've complained for weeks, trying to get him to clean that place up. He's a drunk and just don't care about anything or anyone."

"There's the police now," another woman said.

A couple more neighbors walked up.

Samantha watched as a patrol car parked near Burke's vehicle. One uniformed policeman stepped out and took in the scene. As she watched, a second vehicle pulled in behind the first. It was not a patrol car. She caught her breath as Detective Tuttle got out.

He looked around before heading their way, his gaze resting on her.

She resisted the urge to flee.

"Miss Carr?"

She gave him her most dazzling smile. "Detective Tuttle."

He acknowledged her with a slight nod and then turned to the neighbors as the uniformed officer approached and addressed the situation.

"We're responding to a report of property damages. Which one of you made that call?"

Samantha tried to back away, but Detective Tuttle held up his hand. She checked her watch twice while each of the neighbors told their story. When the voices quieted, she glanced toward them.

They were all looking at her.

Detective Tuttle spoke. "And why are you here, Miss Carr?"

The *Visitor* Has a Ball

Chapter Fifteen

Caught in the Act

Gripped by Tuttle's piercing gaze, Samantha pursed her lips. Why was she here? Curiosity? Wrong place, wrong time? She pulled in a breath. "I'm not sure."

With an exasperated huff, he shook his head. "You head on home, now. I'll be by later."

Like a chastised child, Samantha walked to her car and got in, but she didn't start the car. Not yet. She was torn between wanting to leave and wanting to stay to see what would happen to Burke.

Would he be arrested?

Why did that thought bother her? She was ninety-seven percent sure he had broken into Mom's house not once, but twice. Then he had attempted it again last night. So, wouldn't jail be a good thing?

Her stomach churned all the way home. Something didn't feel right, but she couldn't say what it was, or why.

Her initial response to Burke had been anger. He'd called her a liar, from a family of liars. He was wrong. To her knowledge, no one had lied to him. Mom had assured her that Dad had always shown him patience and kindness.

By the time she pulled in the drive at home, her nerves danced in spiked heels up and down her spine. Emotionally drained, she tugged her purchases from the backseat. Drew's truck sat in the drive, but he was nowhere in sight. Neither was Porter.

The back door was unlocked, so she entered the mudroom and deposited the shopping bags on the counter.

At the sound of voices, she crept into the kitchen and paused. They were in the Florida room. She started to turn away, but something in Mom's voice stopped her.

"Sometimes . . . I still feel as though I can't breathe. You know?"

"I do know," Drew answered. "There's nothing wrong with that. It's your grieving process."

Mom gave a soft sigh. "It's been so long."

"There's no expiration date. No measuring stick. Our emotional processes are as different—as individual as our fingerprints."

Moisture filled Samantha's eyes. Mom sounded so weary. And Samantha should not be listening at the door. It wasn't right.

She turned and tiptoed into the hall where she sank into a chair and stared out the window.

A soft sound drew her focus back to the kitchen where Porter stood in the doorway. Did he sense her heavy heart? When he gave another soft yip, she held out her hand. He approached and sat at her feet.

She leaned forward to pet him. "You're right, as usual. I did something really dumb, and now I'm waiting to see what comes of it."

"What did you do?" Drew's question startled her. She hadn't heard his approach.

She kept her head down. "I'd rather not say." Not to Drew. It was too humiliating.

"That bad, huh?"

She nodded.

He crouched beside her chair. "Well, if you need to talk about it, you have my number. Come on, Porter. Time to go."

Samantha watched as Porter followed his master from the room. Her heart ached in the emptiness they left behind. If only she could go with them, but then Mom would be alone when Detective Tuttle stopped by. Mom was not going to be happy.

Mom's mouth dropped open. "You did what?"

"I thought if he knew, he would stop trying to break in. I realize now, it was stupid of me. I should never have gone over there. I'll probably be chewed out by Detective Tuttle, and I don't blame him."

"Neither do I. That was not a smart move, Samantha. I can't believe you would do something so foolhardy."

When the doorbell rang, Samantha dragged her feet toward the door.

Detective Tuttle tilted his head to the side as he eyed her. "Miss Carr, I'm glad to see you made it home."

"Thank you. Come in. We've been expecting you."

"I won't take much of your time." He stepped inside and followed Samantha into the kitchen where Mom waited.

"May I offer you a cup of coffee, Detective?"

"That would be nice, thank you. I drink it black."

Mom smiled as she filled a cup. "I heard about the fracas this morning with my husband's cousin."

Samantha turned her back and pulled out a couple of chairs at the table.

The back door opened, and Aunt Connie entered. She was on the phone but did a double take when she noticed the detective's presence.

After completing the call, she set her belongings on the counter. "Have you information on the break-in, Detective Tuttle?"

"I was just about to update everyone." He took a seat at the table and opened a notepad.

"There's fresh coffee," Mom said as Aunt Connie joined the circle.

"Thank you. I just finished a cup."

Tuttle took out his phone. "This morning, I received a package from Drew Lindner." He pulled up a photo and showed it to Mom. "Do you recognize this packet of letters?"

Mom's lips parted. "Yes, those were in my husband's box."

Tuttle nodded. "Allegedly, these were found in Burke Woodford's yard, near his trash can. Of course, we can't prove they were found there and even if we could, he could always deny any knowledge of them."

Samantha frowned. "No fingerprints?"

Tuttle tilted his head. "Oh, lots of them. These are old, and who knows how many different people have handled them over the years. No significant match to the prints we have from the window, though."

Samantha huffed out a sigh.

Tuttle eyed her and then turned a page in his notebook and pointed to something. "Burke did complain that he was being harassed by you, Miss Carr. He said you had made multiple visits."

"Multiple visits?" The line in the center of Mom's brow deepened as she glared at Samantha.

"Multiple?"

Samantha bit her lip. Her gaze flitted across the bemused expression on Tuttle's face.

He cleared his throat and shifted in his chair. "Be that as it may, other than accusing three generations of the Carr family of continual lying, he denied everything. Said he was never—at any time—on your property."

Samantha glared at Tuttle. "What?"

Tuttle nodded.

"Furthermore, I spoke at length with Burke's neighbors this morning. The woman whose roses Burke obliterated informed me that he has not been driving his car for the last month or so. He's been dependent on a younger relative—the neighbor thinks he's a nephew—to take him to doctor appointments. And of course, his weekly bingo game." He grinned and turned another page.

Samantha sat forward. "Until last night—you said *he* destroyed the roses—so he was driving the car?"

"The kid never showed. Burke was out of something."

Samantha sniffed. "Something so important, he

had to go out in the wee hours. Because the neighbor told me it was nearly three in the morning when he returned."

"Must have run out of beer," Mom muttered.

Aunt Connie covered her mouth, but her eyes gave away the smile on her lips.

Tuttle shook his head. "I can't comment on that." He emptied his cup and closed his notepad. "Well, ladies, it's been a pleasure, as usual."

Samantha followed him to the door. "I am sorry, Detective."

He turned. "Please, Miss Carr, I think we've passed the formal stage. Your dad and I were friends for many years. You can call me JD." He grinned.

Her shoulders slumped. "Thank you for everything, JD." She ventured a smile. "And you can call me Samantha."

He dipped his head to look at her. "No more visits to the trailer park, Samantha."

She bit back a grin. "Yes, Det—uh—JD."

Bob dashed out of the office as Samantha closed the front door. "Where have you been, silly cat?" She stepped to the door and peeked inside. Someone had packed up the office. The total chaos had been organized into storage containers.

Samantha returned to the kitchen where Mom and Aunt Connie still sat at the table. "Who's been working in the office?"

Mom gave her a smug look. "Drew did most of it. If you had been here, instead of snooping around the trailer park, you could have helped him."

The Visitor Has a Ball

Chapter Sixteen

True Confessions

After one last inventory, Samantha packed the supplies she had assembled for the booth into a couple of canvas tote bags. Outside her bedroom window, storm clouds gathered, darkening the evening sky.

Mom stepped through the open door. "I'm headed to the attic. Aunt Connie said she needs my final approval for the items you two chose for the auction."

Samantha used her foot to slide a bag out of the way. "I'll go with you."

The sound of music and a definite aroma of garlic and olive oil drifted up the stairwell. Aunt Connie had declared it was her night to prepare dinner. Samantha breathed it in. "Whatever she's preparing smells wonderful."

Mom switched on the light. "Yes, it does."

A table against the main wall held the items in question.

Mom fingered one of the Tiffany lamps. "These two lamps sat in Gran's front window for as long as I can remember."

Samantha rubbed her mother's back. "I know. Everything on this table reminds me of her."

Mom picked up an embossed, silver tray. "We stored them in the attic thinking you might like to have them someday. I suppose they're a bit too old-fashioned for you."

Samantha picked up a roll of bubble wrap and cut off a strip. "At this point, I'm still unsure of what I'd like in a home. I do appreciate the thought, though."

Mom dusted one of the Tiffany lamps before removing the shade.

After working in silence for several minutes, Samantha turned to her mother. "What did Burke mean when he said our family lied to him?"

Mom placed the lamp base in the prepared box

and brushed her hands together. "That man is confused about a lot of things. Your father did everything he could to help during a difficult time."

"Like giving Burke Granddad's car?"

"Among other things. It was never enough. Burke's mother poisoned all those kids with her bitterness."

Samantha came to attention. "Why haven't I heard of this before?" She'd known there were cousins nearby, but whenever she had asked about them, someone always changed the subject.

Mom picked up the lampshade and wrapped it with bubble wrap. "While your grandparents were alive, Granddad's sister, Sadie—Burke's mother— was estranged from the family. She had married against her parents' wishes. Her husband was a . . . well, not a nice person. I think he was the one who instigated the whole thing. He insisted Sadie, as the eldest, should have inherited the house, the company, and even that silly baseball. Your great-grandfather was a wise man. He knew Sadie's husband would waste it all. So, he gave Sadie the house she was living in and a small amount of money. That was all. Her brother, your granddad, inherited the bulk of the estate. He took on a couple of partners and made a success of it. When he retired, your father took over as controlling shareholder.

"No doubt, the extended family resented your grandfather's good fortune. I never heard Grandma Carr speak ill of anyone, but she did refer to that side of the family as *bad blood*."

"I don't remember any of that. Well, other than Dad inheriting a share of the company."

"Dad did his best to shield you—us—from anything unpleasant. I do think he experienced guilt to some degree when he became aware of Burke and how the man lived."

"None of that was Dad's fault, though."

"Of course, it wasn't. I told him so, but he had such a good heart. He always wanted to make things better for everyone."

Samantha smiled. "I do remember that."

"I think bringing Burke here that day, and showing him that baseball, was his way of trying to bridge the gap. He had great hopes that Burke would clean himself up . . ."

When her mother's words trailed off, Samantha

looked at her. She seemed far away, lost in thought. "Mom?"

Mom raised her eyes to Samantha's. "I just remembered something."

"What?"

"He told me if Burke would ever quit drinking and make something of his life, he would consider giving him that baseball, to help heal the past." She blinked. "Do you think he told Burke that?"

Aunt Connie's voice echoed in the stairwell. "Hello up there. Dinner's ready."

Samantha pushed aside thoughts of Burke and his family, leaving them for later when she could give her mother's revelations her full consideration.

On Friday morning, high humidity made Samantha's morning jog more of a steam bath. Wringing wet, she trotted around the corner of the house where she all but collided with Drew. He wore a blue shirt, the exact shade of his eyes.

A wide grin on his handsome face, he held up

his hands. "Whoa."

Samantha swiped at a drop of sweat before it rolled into her eye. "Oops, sorry. You're here early."

He held the door open for her. "After you."

Inside the house, she led the way up the stairs. She paused on the second floor. "I'll help as soon as I clean up a little."

"Not necessary. There isn't much. I'll be gone by the time you're out of the shower." He flashed a smile before starting up to the attic.

"Okay, maybe I'll see you later then." She wasn't sure he had heard until he answered her.

"I'll be around to help you assemble your booth."

In her room, Samantha caught a glimpse of herself in the mirror. Yikes. Well, Drew had seen her at her worst, and he hadn't run away or made any snarky remarks. Still, she needed to keep her thoughts well away from him. Maybe he hadn't remarked because he didn't care. She blew out a sigh. Ignoring him was not going to be easy.

Samantha rushed through her shower to no avail. When she looked out her window, Drew's truck was gone. She ran her fingers through her still damp hair, twisted it into a bun on top of her head, and finished her makeup. After checking her phone for messages, she headed downstairs.

While Mom and Aunt Connie finished getting ready, Samantha made smoothies for the three of them to drink on the way.

Samantha resolved to keep her focus on the day ahead, and far away from Burke and the mahogany box. Should be easy enough. Especially if a certain hunky landscaper was on site.

Drew unloaded the last box from the bed of his pickup as they arrived.

Aunt Connie stepped out of the car and into her management role, sending everyone in different directions.

Samantha was happy to have a job that would keep her busy most of the day. She caught Drew's eye and smiled.

He responded with a cool nod.

What was up with that? Samantha's brow furrowed as her mind replayed their conversation at home. Had she said something to offend him?

Drew joined her beside the tables that would become her booth. "Just tell me what you need me to do."

Samantha cast a glance around the room. There was a definite chill in the air. She opened her plan book and pointed. "This is what I'm going to end up with."

He shrugged. "Looks pretty straightforward."

She had expected a compliment, awe at her artistic design, anything except his blah comment.

He turned his back and positioned three of the tables in a straight line.

She covered those with white cotton tablecloths and then showed him where she wanted the window frame.

The old frame was six feet tall by three feet wide. She wanted it set on its side on the middle table. They blocked it into place.

Drew stood back, shaking his head.

"What?"

"It's unstable."

"We can prop it against the wall."

"If someone bumps the table, it could be disastrous." After a moment's hesitation, he turned toward the door. "I'll be right back."

She watched his retreating figure. "Okay." She

stayed busy on the other tables until he returned several minutes later, wearing a leather tool belt and carrying a black canvas bag.

Samantha organized the other elements for her design, while keeping Drew's activities in her peripheral vision.

He set the bag on a nearby chair and removed several metal brackets and some clamps. Then he lifted the window and laid it on the floor. He installed a bracket on either end, finishing with one in the middle. Afterward, he lifted the frame and centered it on the tables. He looked up at her. "I could use your help now."

She joined him behind the tables to hold the frame in place as he applied the clamps. "I see what you're doing. I'm so glad you're here. I never would have thought to do that."

"Right."

She blew out a pent-up breath. "OK, what's the problem?"

He fastened the final clamp, straightened to his full height, and looked down at her. "No problem, now."

"Yes, there is. Maybe you don't want to be

here? Have I done something to offend you?"

Still looking down at her, he leaned against the wall. "Did you go back over to that trailer yesterday?"

She blinked. How had he found out—Mom—Aunt Connie? No sense denying it. She nodded. "Go ahead, you may as well chew me out, too."

His lips quirked. "So that's the dumb thing you were talking to Porter about. I'm sure you've heard it from everyone, but, Samantha, that was . . ." he huffed out a breath.

"Foolish?"

"You're not helping the case, and you could've gotten into a lot of trouble. If Tuttle hadn't come along when he did . . ."

"Ah, so it was Detective Tuttle who told you."

"I called him to ask about the letters."

"And he talked about the case? Isn't that like breaking protocol or something?"

He shook his head and chuckled. "I suppose it would be, but he's a friend, and he was concerned about you."

"And this is a small town. Everyone knows everyone else's business." *Too sharp, Samantha.*

Turning away, she picked up a length of sky-blue cloth and began draping it over the back of the window frame. When she faced the front again, Drew had gone.

The Visitor Has a Ball

Chapter Seventeen

Turn of Event

Blinking back tears, Samantha finished draping the cloth. Deep breath. Exhale. Relax. She could not allow herself to be distracted at this point. There was too much going on that needed her full awareness.

Mom. Aunt Connie. The gala. The mahogany box. Burke.

No time for foolish crushes.

She finished the display before backing away to get the full effect.

Aunt Connie looked up from her seating chart. "Oh, Samantha, it turned out even better than I imagined. Eva Grace, come and look at this."

Mom turned from her work at one of the round tables in the center of the room. She walked toward them, taking it in. "Oh, my. This is delightful, Samantha."

Aunt Connie grasped Samantha's hand. "Let's take a lunch break."

"Where's Drew? Did he leave without saying goodbye?"

Mom's question pierced Samantha's heart. She fought to keep her mind on the display. "Not sure. I guess he had work or somewhere else to be."

Mom rubbed her hands together and sighed. "That's so unlike him."

Aunt Connie took Mom's hand. "I'm sure we'll hear from him later. Come on, let's go."

Samantha's steps lagged as she followed Mom and Aunt Connie from the room. The last thing she had ever wanted to do was to alienate a fine man who could have been someone important.

After lunch, Samantha helped Mom set up the dining tables. Each table sat eight, and there were fifteen tables arranged around the room.

Aunt Connie completed the seating chart. "The flower arrangements will be delivered in the morning. After the caterers set the tables, we can place the name cards."

"I can't believe the gala is almost here." Mom shook out another white tablecloth and smoothed it onto a table.

One of the other volunteers stepped through the atrium door. "Ms. Wright, the workers have finished the platform and need your approval."

Aunt Connie followed the woman.

When the front door opened, Samantha turned to look. Was it Drew? Her shoulders slumped at the sight of JD Tuttle striding toward them.

He lifted his hand in greeting.

Mom came to stand beside Samantha and whispered, "I hope he has good news."

"Afternoon, Miz Carr, Samantha." He stood with his feet apart, crossed his arms over his chest, and took in the room. "Looks like you're almost ready for the gala."

Mom nodded. "It's coming along. How are you, JD?"

"I'm well, thank you. I won't take too much of

your time, I know you're busy. We had a bit of a breakthrough on the case this morning, so I thought I'd fill you in. We picked up a certain person of interest. It's a sensitive situation because we're dealing with a juvenile, but this particular individual's prints match what we found at the scene." JD's eyebrows arched as his lips curved into a smile.

Samantha gave a quick intake of breath. She had no problem following JD's hints. He had to be talking about Burke's underage nephew.

Mom didn't hesitate. "Are you talking about Burke's nephew, Rory?"

JD held up his hand. "I will neither confirm nor deny."

Samantha stared at her mother. How did Mom know this boy's name when Samantha hadn't even been aware of his existence until talking to Burke's neighbors? Trying to keep the scowl off her face, she switched her gaze back to JD.

"The kid clammed up at first, but when I reminded him how slow the system works and how he'd most likely be of age by the time this whole thing gets settled, he was happy to make a deal." He finished with a grin.

Questions crowded and fell over one another in Samantha's mind. "So, did Burke coerce his nephew, or was it all the boy's idea?"

"Again, I will neither confirm nor deny any specific party." JD rubbed the back of his neck. "All we know right now is, the kid has confessed to entering your home on at least two occasions. He swears that last attempt wasn't him."

Samantha thought back to what she knew had happened. "That would line up with what Burke's neighbors . . . I mean, a certain person's neighbors . . . said about him driving that night."

JD nodded.

A shaft of hope pierced Samantha's heart. "So, can you search Burke's trailer, now?"

"I've applied for a warrant for a certain property that might hold stolen merchandise. And a concerned citizen organized a cleanup crew to clear the trash."

Samantha glanced at her mom. "If the letters were there, then maybe there is other evidence."

JD shrugged. "Nothing so far, but the neighbors are happy about the cleanup."

Samantha huffed. "I'll bet."

JD's phone rang. He excused himself and strode toward the door. "No kidding?"

When the door slammed behind his retreating back, Samantha exchanged glances with Mom.

Aunt Connie brisked in from the atrium. A bright smile twinkled her eyes. She lifted her hands in the air and then pressed them against her chest. "The platform is perfect. And we have our final head count. We are sold out. This is turning out to be one of our best. On top of all that, I just got a call from the mayor. He asked if there is any way we can squeeze in another table to accommodate some out-of-town guests of his. What do you think?"

She glanced from Samantha's face to Mom's and then back at her. "What's going on? Did I miss something?"

Before Samantha could answer, JD reentered and drew all their attention.

He shook his head. "This day keeps getting better. Sorry, but I have to take off. Miss Samantha, can you walk out with me?"

Samantha's curiosity kicked into high gear as she followed JD. What did he have to tell her that couldn't be said in front of Mom and Aunt Connie?

Once they were outside, JD spoke. "That was Drew on the phone. He's over at Burke's helping with the cleanup. He was weed eating around the base of the trailer when a section of the underpinning collapsed, and he caught sight of something."

JD halted beside his vehicle. "He thinks it's the box."

Samantha caught her breath. "Can I go with you?"

JD shook his head. "Not a good idea, hon. Burke will be back home soon. He's at the bingo hall on Friday afternoons. Never misses. You shouldn't be anywhere near there when he returns. Besides, we can't touch anything without that warrant. I'll call as soon as I know more."

Samantha stood in the parking lot as JD drove away. When her phone pinged twice, she ignored it. All she could think about was how Drew had left here and gone to Burke's to help with cleanup.

If she hadn't gone over to Burke's yesterday, and alienated Drew, he may have kept her in the loop.

Mom opened the door. "I've been texting you. What's going on?"

Samantha turned and walked back inside. Should she tell Mom and risk disappointment if it turned out to be nothing?

"JD heard from the crew doing clean up at Burke's trailer. They didn't find anything else in the trash, so he's going to check on the warrant. Once he has that, he can do a more in-depth search."

Mom seemed fine with that explanation. "Well, he could have told *us* that, silly man. Now, come back inside and help. Aunt Connie figured out how to squeeze in another table."

Chapter Eighteen

Invitation to the Ball

Aunt Connie had gone out for dinner with one of the Wright Foundation's local supporters, so Samantha and her mom sat at the breakfast bar for a quick supper of salad and fruit.

Mom dabbed at her lips with a napkin. "What a day we've had."

Before Samantha could answer, the doorbell rang. She slid off the stool. "Looks like it's not over yet."

Expecting—hoping—to find Drew at the door, she exhaled at the sight of JD Tuttle. Again. *What now?*

Maybe they had identified the box. Samantha stood aside for him to enter.

He didn't come in but stepped to one side.

Her eyes on JD's face, Samantha joined him on the porch.

He spoke in a low voice. "I need a favor from you and your mother if she's home."

Samantha glanced over her shoulder as Mom approached the door. "JD wants to speak to both of us."

Mom stepped onto the porch where they stood facing JD.

About that time, Drew pulled into the drive and stopped near the front walk. The truck's passenger-side door swung open, and a teenage boy got out.

Samantha stepped closer to the porch railing. Was this Rory? She watched JD's face, wondering what he had in mind.

"What's he doing here, JD?" Mom's soft-spoken question pierced Samantha's heart.

Drew, followed by Porter, joined the young man beside the truck.

JD answered Mom loud enough to be heard by all of them. "Rory has something he wants to say to you."

Mom crossed her arms over her chest and sent

Samantha a wary look.

Obeying a command from his master, Porter trotted up the steps and perched beside Mom, leaning his body against her leg.

Her frown vanished as she reached down to pat his head.

Drew and the boy strode up the walk. Rory was much younger and smaller than Samantha had expected. At least a foot shorter than Drew, he had shoulder-length hair that hung in clumps. He kept pushing at it as they walked and then stood with his head down until JD prompted him. "It's all right, Rory."

Drew took up a relaxed stance behind the boy but made no eye contact with Samantha.

Pangs of guilt stabbed her heart. He wouldn't even look at her.

Rory ran the back of his hand across his lips and glanced up. His gaze connected briefly with Mom and Samantha. "I'm sorry for all the trouble."

JD nodded. "And?"

Rory pulled in a breath, his eyes on Mom. "I'm sorry I broke into your house and took that box."

When Mom heaved a sigh, JD spoke to her in a

low voice. "This was his idea, Miz Carr. He wanted to do it. He wants to make it right."

Mom nodded and spoke to Rory. "I accept your apology."

Rory bowed his head and uttered a barely audible, "Thank you, ma'am."

JD descended the steps. "All right, young man, let's go."

Her eyes pleading, Mom looked at Samantha.

Gripping the porch railing, Samantha leaned forward. "What will happen now, JD?"

The two men paused.

Rory hung back as JD spoke.

"I'm going to work with his lawyer, and we'll try to talk the judge into community service."

"Do you think he'll agree—the judge, I mean."

JD gripped Rory's shoulder. "It is a first offense. If we can get Burke to admit it was his idea, that would go a long way toward clearing up this mess."

Burke's unpleasant scowl plagued Samantha's memory. She pulled in a breath and released it. "What if he won't?"

He lifted his hand from Rory's shoulder and

looked at Samantha. "There's still a pretty good chance. I'm sure he'd appreciate knowing y'all are praying for him."

Mom stepped close to Samantha. "We will be praying, and I'll be happy to write a letter if needed."

Rory bowed his head and reached up to push the hair from his face.

JD flashed a smile. "Thank you, Miz Carr. That would be helpful." He turned and walked toward his vehicle with Rory.

Drew hung around after JD left with the boy.

Mom invited him inside, but he declined. "I need to get home. But I was wondering if I could speak to Samantha."

Mom smiled into Samantha's eyes. "Of course." She turned, walked inside, and closed the door.

Porter's focus stayed fixed on his master until Drew gave a soft whistle and ordered him to the truck.

As Samantha stepped down from the porch, Drew spoke. "I'm sorry I rushed off this morning without saying good-bye."

"And I'm sorry I was sharp with you. I suppose

by now, you may have noticed my habit of blurting out whatever is on my mind, only to regret it soon after."

Drew dipped his head and grinned. "I have noticed that, yes."

She bit her lip and peered up at him. That grin, though. "Maybe I need therapy."

"Ha. I think that can be arranged. I'll put you on Porter's wait list."

Samantha laughed out loud. "So, I'm forgiven?"

"We'll call it even at this point." He stuck his hands in his pockets and leaned ever-so-slightly forward to gaze into her face. "I was wondering if you'd like to be my date tomorrow night."

Keeping her eyes on his, Samantha took a moment to bask in the thrill his words created. "Hmm, I don't know. It's a bit late to ask."

He tilted his head. "You know I'm pretty good at reading people."

"I'm a bad liar. My face always gives me away."

"So, is that a yes?"

She wanted to play it cool, stay aloof, anything

except melt in his presence like a giant pat of butter. But why shouldn't she just go with the flow for once? *Que sera* and all that. *Head up, deep breath.* "Yes, Drew, I would love to be your date tomorrow night."

His lips curved in a slow smile. "Great. I'll pick you up at seven."

Samantha watched until the truck's taillights disappeared at the end of the street. Had he just asked her out on a date? Not just any date—the gala—the social event of the season. She'd be the envy of every single lady in attendance.

She looked up at the evening sky. The soft night air held a heady scent of sweetness from Mom's night-blooming jasmine. She wasn't ready to go back inside, so she strolled to the back garden. In the waning light, she noticed Mom sitting in the gazebo.

Samantha joined her.

Mom laid her hand on Samantha's wrist. "Is everything all right with you and Drew?"

You and Drew. The words sent another thrill through Samantha's heart, followed by a warning. She closed her eyes. "Yes, everything is fine. He wanted to—he asked me to be his date tomorrow night."

Samantha looked up but couldn't see Mom's face. Her quick intake of breath revealed excitement. "Oh, I'm so happy for you. He's such a nice young man."

Samantha bit her lip. *Don't get too attached too soon.* She wanted to warn Mom. Protect her from further disappointment. Samantha's dating history had not been a stellar one. She tended to make bad choices. "Mom, I . . ."

"Sweetheart, don't let past mistakes overshadow what God is doing in your life right now." She took Samantha's hand in both of hers. "You need to forgive yourself and then let it go."

Her biggest mistake—a man she'd met in college who had promised her the world but had used her to gain his way into her father's company. A man whose greed almost destroyed Samantha's relationship with Dad. Tears blurred her eyes at the memory.

Mom squeezed her hand. "Let it go. Dad and I forgave you. Forgive yourself."

Samantha swiped at a drop of moisture that had managed to escape. She pulled in a deep breath and released it. "I'm trying, Mom. I really am." She leaned against her mother's shoulder.

Mom kissed the top of her head. "You'll get there."

Two bright beams of light announced Aunt Connie's return.

Samantha sat forward and smiled. "I love you, Mom."

Mom caressed her cheek. "I love you, too, sweetheart."

Arm-in-arm, they walked toward the house to meet Aunt Connie, who waited beside the back door. "Did I miss anything?"

The Visitor Has a Ball

Chapter Nineteen

Caged Bull

Samantha's phone announced a text message. She was running late but took a minute to look. It was from JD.

Positive ID on the box. Will have to hold on to it for now.

She shoved the phone back into her purse and grabbed the keys. She'd forgotten all about the box last night but maybe it was just as well. It was evidence, so the police would have to hold onto it until this whole ordeal was over. How long would it take?

She hugged Mom on the way out of the door. "Thanks for lunch. I'll see you in a couple of hours."

Mom tucked a stray lock of hair behind

Samantha's ear. "Drive carefully."

Samantha smiled into her eyes. Should she slow down, take a moment to tell Mom the news? Another ping of her phone cinched it. Aunt Connie's number.

Where are you?

The event venue hummed with activity by the time Samantha arrived. The florist flitted from table to table like a butterfly as she added finishing touches to the pink, white, and lavender centerpieces.

The caterers moved about the room, amid the soft clink of cutlery and glassware. Samantha's gaze lit on Aunt Connie as she brisked from one spot to the next, blithely checking items off her to-do list. She looked up when Samantha entered the hall. "There you are. Come and take a gander at the auction table."

When Samantha walked over, her aunt pointed out a couple of late entries. "A spa day at *NuYu Salon* and a weekend at the Kentucky Castle."

Samantha clasped her hands. "The Castle? That will draw a lot of interest."

Aunt Connie's head bobbed. "Yes. I got that

one last night. Talk about under the wire. Have you heard from Uncle Paul?"

Samantha shook her head. "No, but Mom said not to worry. They're always late."

"She's right. They are. That's why I thought it was best for her to stay home today."

When one of the caterers called her name, Aunt Connie scurried off.

Samantha stood back and surveyed the auction booth and then rechecked each sign-up sheet, making sure all the information was correct and the pens functioned.

Behind her, the front door opened and shut. So many were going in and out, Samantha paid no heed, until she heard a loud crash followed by an exclamation from Aunt Connie.

"What do you think you're doing? You are not authorized to be in here."

Samantha turned just in time to see Burke's bulky tattooed arm reach for a second table. She dashed toward him and grabbed the back of his dirty tee shirt. Two of the caterers, a young man, and a young woman, tried to grab his arms, but Burke fought them off, knocking the young woman into one of the other tables.

Someone had to do something before Burke destroyed the entire room and days of labor.

Samantha stepped between him and the table and slapped at his big paw of a hand. "Stop it, Burke."

He eyed her with a hate-filled sneer. "I don't have to do what you say, you . . . you . . ."

At that moment, Aunt Connie stepped beside Samantha and jabbed at Burke's chest with her finger. "You heard her. Stop. This. Now."

Samantha wanted to laugh out loud at the look on her aunt's face, but before she could react, several of the other workers gathered beside them, pressing in on Burke until he took a backward step.

He raised his head like an angry bull and held his fists up as though he might charge all of them.

The front door swung open again. Two policemen rushed forward. Within moments, they had Burke handcuffed.

Aunt Connie pulled up a nearby chair and sat down.

Samantha joined her at the table, noting her flushed face. "Are you okay?"

Aunt Connie nodded. "I'll recover. What about you?"

"I'm all right." She turned to one of the officers as he finished reading the man his rights. "How did you get here so fast?"

"One of his neighbors called to report that he had taken off. We just happened to be in the area. Saw him turn into the parking lot."

Aunt Connie blew out a relieved breath. "Well, someone needs to take his car away."

Burke spewed. "I told you they were trying to take back that car. Bunch of lying . . ."

JD Tuttle walked through the open door. "Can it, Burke. Else we'll lock you up for good."

Aunt Connie stood and laid an open palm over her chest. "Thank you, JD. I thought we were going to have to start all over in here."

JD shook his head as he took in the damage. "I am so sorry about this. I had no idea he'd take off again." He turned to the waiting officers. "This is his third DUI. Take him downtown. I'll be in shortly to process the arrest. Have the car towed to impound so he can't get away again."

He faced Aunt Connie and Samantha. "Tell me

what I can do to help."

Aunt Connie shrugged and glanced around.

Already the workers were beginning to clean up the broken glass. The florist was salvaging the flowers from the centerpiece, and someone else was setting up a new table to replace the broken one. Even the woman who had been shoved seemed to be all right. She spread a clean tablecloth over the new table.

Aunt Connie smoothed her hands down her suit. "It looks as though we have it all in hand. At least no one's hurt."

The head caterer stepped over. "Don't you worry about it, Miss Wright. We'll have it all set back up in no time."

The florist patted Aunt Connie's arm. "And the flowers aren't a total loss. Nothing I can't fix."

Aunt Connie turned back to JD. "We are indeed fine here."

JD nodded. "Good."

One of the workers gestured. "A question for you, Ms. Wright."

With a nod, Aunt Connie stepped away.

JD turned to Samantha and tipped his head

toward the auction booth. "Let's walk over that way and let these folks get their work done."

Samantha followed JD, who stopped beside the auction table.

"I just left your house. As I told your mother, Burke is still denying any wrongdoing. Even though the boy wrote up and signed a confession, Burke maintains he knew nothing about any of it."

Samantha shook her head. "So, he's laying all the blame on Rory?"

"He is as mean and stubborn as a mule with a toothache."

Samantha smiled at the saying. "So, what happens now?"

"Well, your mother told me she doesn't want Burke to go to jail. He's old and sick. She wanted me to ask him to do the right thing. If he would return your daddy's property, she'd drop the charges."

Drop the charges? "Huh. What do you think about that?"

He pressed his lips into a tight frown before answering. "She's right about him being sick. I don't think he'd live long in jail. At the same time, the man needs to pay for what he's done. He used that boy and could have ruined his life. That poor kid was miserable, thinking Burke was going to turn on him. I don't know what all Burke told him, but he had the boy convinced he could make the rest of his life a living you-know-what."

Samantha knew exactly what. And she didn't doubt Burke's ability to make good on that threat.

JD looked at several of the auction items before he continued. "I'm positive your dad wouldn't want to press charges. He did everything he could to help old Burke." He rapped the table with his knuckles. "But I think he would have been mighty disappointed in the man. There is an end to patience for most folks. Anyway, I said all that to catch you up to speed, and I also wanted to ask your opinion. After what happened here today, should I offer to drop the charges if he returns that baseball?"

Samantha thought for a moment. The memory of Burke's sneering expression made her blood boil. He was a creep. That was for sure. But, like JD said, Dad would've given grace. It had been his way, and no doubt, it was her mother's plan to honor Dad's memory. Samantha could do no less. "If he owns up to it and returns the baseball."

JD stuck his hands in his pockets. "I figured you'd say that. Still, I had to check. I'll take care of it then. Either way, we're going to keep him under surveillance. He won't blow his nose without us knowing it. We'll get the neighbors involved. They're the ones who reported him leaving in the car today."

As JD walked away, Samantha thought about what he'd told her—not the part about Burke—but about Mom not wanting Burke to go to jail. Mom, who had seen his character from the beginning. She had even seemed to despise him. What had changed?

Love covers a multitude of sins . . .

There it was again. That still, small voice. Samantha pondered. Does Mom love Burke? Not as a suitor, but as a human being.

Could Samantha do the same? Forgive the man for what he'd done?

The *Visitor* Has a Ball

Chapter Twenty

Mutt-n-Tux

As she drove home, Samantha struggled with her conscience. That man was hateful and spiteful, but he was also sick and weak. Just the kind of person Jesus would reach out to with healing and forgiveness. She pulled into the driveway but didn't open the door.

Instead, she laid her palm against her chest and drew a breath. On her exhale, she whispered a prayer. "Yahweh. Father, I forgive him. I forgive Burke."

In that moment, she was free. Samantha. Not Burke. Tears coursed down her cheeks as she wept.

The house was quiet when Samantha entered. Mom's bedroom door was closed. She was probably napping. In her room, she pushed her keys inside her purse. Something sharp poked her fingertip. She extracted it and looked at Mr. Mitchell's business card.

She set her purse on the dresser and stared at her reflection in the mirror. Then she tucked the card into the edge of the mirror frame. She'd call him on Monday after the gala and hear what he had to offer. She stood still a moment. Moving back home—was she actually considering that? Hope stirred her heart. She closed her eyes and whispered a prayer. *Your will be done, Lord.*

After a refreshing shower, Samantha sat in the window seat to do her nails.

Her hair was still wet when Drew called, igniting a flurry of emotions in her midsection. Why was he calling? Her throat rivaled the Sahara Desert as she croaked out, "Hello?"

Surely, he wasn't going to beg off.

"Is there any way I can pick you up a little early?"

Her hand flew to her wet hair. "How early?"

"Maybe six-thirty?"

"Um, yes, I guess that would be all right." Dare

she ask why?

"Great. I'll explain when I get there."

"Okay." She ended the call and blew on her nails. No time for a last coat. Two would have to do. She jumped up and ran to the bathroom, where she removed the hairdryer from its place, careful not to mar the fresh nail polish.

After drying her hair, she smoothed it with a flat iron and then gathered it into a French twist with wispy curls at each ear.

At six-twenty-five, the doorbell rang. She slipped the dress over her head and settled it into place. The satiny white color of the dress accentuated her sun-kissed complexion. The silver threads woven into a swirling pattern embellished with white and peacock blue beads, sparkled in the lamplight and kicked up a flurry of excitement in her midsection.

She fastened on a sapphire necklace, earrings, and a matching bracelet—a gift from her father for her twenty-first birthday.

A soft knock at her door and Mom's voice calling her name sent Samantha into a panic. She inhaled and eased out a breath while slipping her shoes on. "I'm ready."

Mom opened the door. She shook her head and smiled. "Oh, Samantha. You look lovely."

Samantha picked up her clutch and stepped into the hall. "I don't think I was this excited about prom."

"You weren't. Remember who your date was?"

Samantha grimaced. "Rodney Simpson. Why did I let him talk me into going to the prom? Now, forever I have those memories."

Mom snickered. "And I have the photos to prove it."

"I asked you to throw those away." As Samantha descended the stairs with Mom following close behind, every other thought flew away at the sight of her date waiting in the foyer. Drew wore a black tuxedo, crisp white shirt, and black bow tie.

Admiration flashed in his clear, blue eyes as he shook his head. "Wow."

Beside him, Porter stood and wagged his tail.

Samantha covered her mouth. The dog was wearing a tux. Laughter bubbled and spilled over.

Porter yipped.

Drew chuckled. "What's the matter? Have you

never seen a dog in a tux?"

At the base of the stairs, Samantha reached to pat the dog's head. "I have never. He looks like a giant penguin. A very cute one." She straightened. "Where on earth did you find this thing?"

"At the supply store. You can find most anything for dogs these days."

Mom interrupted them. "Pictures." She held up her phone. "Stand in front of the fireplace. You too, Porter."

Drew arched his brows at Samantha. "The main reason I needed to arrive early."

After several poses, he held up his hand. "We need to go. We don't want to be late."

Samantha gave him a sideways glance, but he was already headed for the door.

"To the truck, Porter."

The dog scurried out.

Mom waved. "I'll see you soon."

Samantha paused. "Have you heard from Uncle Paul and Teagan?"

"They were delayed but should be here any minute. Don't worry about me. Just go and have fun."

As they walked to the truck, Drew smiled down at Samantha. "You look so amazing. I wish I had thought to rent a limo."

Joy swelled, warming her insides. "Your truck is fine."

He helped her settle in, taking extra care with the hem of her dress.

Porter sat beside her, looking like a dog-prince. All he needed was a crown.

Drew got in and started the engine. "I've had a busy afternoon, but I didn't want to disappoint your mom. She sent me a text about taking pictures."

Samantha made a mental note to find and destroy the prom photos as soon as possible. A grin on Drew's face ignited her curiosity. Something was up.

"I have a funny story to tell you." He kept his attention on the road as he navigated through evening traffic.

"The other day when I was at Burke's, I talked to his next-door neighbor. I mentioned I had installed an alarm system for someone, and the guy asked if I could do something similar for him. He wanted a couple of cameras on Burke's side of his trailer so he could keep an eye on things over there."

Samantha smiled and shook her head. "And of course, you agreed to do it, Mr. Fix-it."

He nodded. "Of course. It didn't take long, just a few minutes. I got him all set up. So, this morning, he called and said the cameras kept beeping and wondered if I could stop by and make an adjustment."

"Which you did."

He grinned. "It was on my way. I arrived—we arrived—all dressed up and caused quite a stir among the neighbors."

Samantha laughed and scratched Porter's ears. "Did you cause a spectacle?"

"He did more than that. While I was making the adjustments to the neighbor's security app, the camera came on again. There was Porter, on camera, sniffing around Burke's trailer like he was after something. He followed whatever the smell was to Burke's porch and scratched at the door."

Samantha's jaw went slack. "He didn't."

Drew chuckled. "Yes, he did. So, Burke opens the door, and finds a dog in a tuxedo, sitting on his porch."

Samantha opened her eyes wide. "Oh no."

"Oh, yes. We sat there watching on camera as Burke opened the door, stared at Porter, closed the door, and opened it again. After Burke closed his door a second time, I jumped up and gave Porter his truck command from the neighbor's window. When Burke opened the door one more time, Porter had disappeared. Burke came out, looked all around, and then went back inside. Al—the neighbor—almost cried he laughed so hard."

Samantha giggled. "That is a funny story." After a moment's thought, she looked at Porter. "What scent do you think he picked up?"

Drew rubbed the dog's head. "Could have been anything. Most likely rats. The place was a mess for a long time."

Samantha smoothed the silky fur around Porter's ears. "I'm just glad Burke didn't try to hurt him."

At the mansion, Drew pulled into the line for valet parking. "I don't think Burke is violent. He's just an angry alcoholic."

Samantha wanted to disagree with Drew's opinion of Burke. He hadn't seen the man's outburst, but maybe that was a conversation for a different day.

Drew got out and handed his keys to the valet. A volunteer stepped forward and opened the door for Samantha. She hesitated until Drew stepped alongside and offered his hand.

When Porter hopped down, everyone standing nearby stopped talking for a moment and stared.

Samantha stifled a giggle. "What's the matter? Have y'all never seen a dog wearing a tux?"

The Visitor Has a Ball

Chapter Twenty-One

All in the Family

Samantha waited while Drew clipped on Porter's leash and handed it to a young man in a black suit.

When he returned to her side, Samantha gave him a questioning look.

He shrugged. "There is no way I was going to let Porter steal the limelight. Not with a gorgeous woman like you on my arm." A wide grin lit his countenance.

Whoa. Samantha wanted to find the nearest ceiling fan and step beneath it. "But he is coming in? If not, he'd be all dressed up with nowhere to go."

Drew chuckled, took her hand, and led her forward. "My friend, Joe is taking him for a walk first."

Samantha had to admit that the admiration they received upon entering was nice. The dress had been a good choice. Her date was an even better one.

Aunt Connie's cranberry red off-shoulder gown made her easy to locate. She spotted them and came over. "You two look elegant. Please tell me your mother remembered to get pictures."

"Oh, she did." Samantha wanted to say more, but Aunt Connie was called away.

Drew left her side to meet Porter at the door.

Samantha tugged the phone from her clutch and snapped a couple of pics as the two made a grand entrance amid laughter and applause. This was a shining moment for them. Samantha shook her head. Drew and Porter Wagger had become local celebrities.

Almost half an hour passed before Mom entered on Uncle Paul's arm with Samantha's cousin Teagan on the other side of her father. She made a beeline for Samantha when she saw her.

Samantha met her halfway and gave her a warm hug. "I have missed you so much."

Teagan stepped back. "I've missed you, too."

Her eyes widened. "Your dress is awesome."

Samantha smoothed her hand down the front of her gown. "Isn't it? But look at you, all dolled up."

The girl's eyes sparkled behind her glasses. "The dress was a gift from Aunt Connie."

"It suits you perfectly. Come meet my date." Teagan's hand in hers, she led her to Drew. "This is my cousin Teagan. More like the little sister I never had."

Drew took Teagan's hand. "It's a pleasure to meet you."

Teagan's awed expression reminded Samantha of her first encounter with Drew. He was a stunner.

He led them to their table and held a chair for Teagan and then for Samantha.

Porter waited beside Drew's chair until his master whispered a command. "At ease, buddy." He lay down but kept his head up as if on alert.

Mitzi Chandler and her husband, Bob, filled out their table of eight. Mom and Mitzi talked nonstop for the first ten minutes of the meal.

Samantha blinked away tears. It was so good to see Mom back to her old self as though the depression and pain of the last year and a half had never existed.

But it had. And the man who sat next to Samantha had been integral in drawing her mom back into life. Of course, he would give Porter most of the credit.

Drew leaned so close that his lips brushed her hair. "It's great to see your mother so animated."

Samantha had to agree. "I was thinking the same thing. At one time, I wondered if she'd ever recover." She reached to pat Porter's head.

The dog looked up at her, his soulful eyes adoring.

During dinner, Aunt Connie stood on stage and introduced the first of several entertainers, a comedian who kept everyone laughing as he shared stories of family life. His act was followed by a local country singer who reminded everyone to stop by the silent auction booth. "I put my bid in on that weekend at the castle. It would make a great anniversary gift for my beloved."

A short and entertaining video of the horse-riding event at Briarbeck's came next, and then Aunt Connie introduced the children. They received a standing ovation for their performance of *My Old*

Kentucky Home.

Aunt Connie joined in the applause before returning to the microphone. "Aren't they amazing? Their artwork is on display in the front lobby. During the break, I hope you'll take a few minutes to admire it."

Drew got up and clipped on Porter's leash. "I'm going to take Porter and visit with the children for a few minutes." As he straightened, the band began to play. He winked at Samantha. "Save me a dance."

Samantha's cheeks warmed. She used her fork to push crumbs around on her plate to help calm her nerves.

A familiar voice broke into her thoughts. JD stood with Aunt Connie. "Evening, Miz Carr, Samantha." He nodded to the other occupants of the table.

Mom smiled and indicated Drew's vacant chair. "Hello, JD. Won't you join us?"

Aunt Connie returned to her seat. "I found him admiring the children's artwork and invited him over."

JD looked dapper in a black suit, white shirt, and black tie. As he pulled out the chair, he nodded toward Porter and Drew. "I've seen everything now. That pooch is dressed better than I am."

Samantha laughed. "I think you look very handsome tonight, JD."

He surprised her with a blush. "Thank you, Samantha. I appreciate that."

Mom introduced JD to Uncle Paul and Teagan. "Of course, you already know Bob and Mitzi Chandler."

JD shook hands with Uncle Paul and nodded to Bob. "Good to see you, Bob, Mitzi."

After a few minutes of polite chitchat, JD turned to Mom. "I wanted to stop by and let you both know that Burke has returned the baseball." His gaze connected with Samantha's.

Aunt Connie reached for Mom's hand. "Oh, Eva Grace, isn't that wonderful news?"

Her lips trembled as Mom nodded. "Thank the Lord. I prayed he'd do the right thing."

JD grinned. "Funny you should say that. When I stopped at Burke's this evening, he was ranting about seeing a dog in a tuxedo—said it was snooping around his trailer. I thought the man had slipped off his rocker 'til I saw it for myself." He nodded to the front where Drew and Porter interacted with the children.

Samantha beamed as everyone at their table responded with smiles and laughter.

JD continued his story. "After he calmed down a bit, I told him what you said, that you would drop the charges if he would give back what he took. I said, 'Burke, do the right thing for once.' Then I gave him the note like you asked me to. I never thought he'd do it. In fact, he closed the door in my face. I was about to leave when he cracked the door wide enough to pass me the baseball. 'Take it and get on out of here,' he said."

Curiosity etched a hole in Samantha's concentration. She would have to ask Mom about that note later. She looked at JD. "So, you have the baseball?"

He nodded. "It's evidence, of course, along with the mahogany box. I'll make sure you get them both back as soon as possible."

Aunt Connie came to attention. "What did you say about the box?"

JD propped his elbows on the table and leaned toward Mom. "I never told you about the box, did

I?"

Mom shook her head. "No, you did not."

"Well, there was a reason for that. The box was found beneath Burke's trailer when a section of the underpinning got knocked down by the cleanup crew. It was delivered to the office and when it was examined, we found a significant stash of . . . a controlled substance."

Samantha's jaw dropped. "In the box?"

JD nodded. Speaking in a low voice, he went on. "When we questioned Rory about it, he denied any knowledge of it. Then, after he thought about it, he got a look on his face. When I pressed him, he admitted that Burke had some dealings with a sketchy character soon after he'd sold the silver coins at a pawn shop. He ordered the boy to stay in the car. The kid said he couldn't see anything since they were standing behind the vehicle with the trunk open. He thinks maybe Burke stuffed the goods inside the box at that time. But he never allowed the boy access to the trunk or the box."

Something pinged Samantha's memory. Porter sniffing around the trailer. Was he after a rat, or had he picked up the scent of narcotics?

Mom's brow creased. "JD, since you found that controlled substance in his possession, does that mean Burke will have to go to jail?"

JD sat back and tilted his head to the side. "Well, it will be up to the judge. I can't say for certain, but I expect he'll end up on house arrest. Something like that."

Samantha reached in front of JD to take Mom's hand. "Can I ask about the note, Mom, or is it none of my business?"

Mom shrugged. "It was just three words, but I pray he never forgets them." She squeezed Samantha's hand and smiled. "I forgive you."

A glow of warmth spread through Samantha's entire being. Everything was going to be all right.

Aunt Connie left her seat to stand behind Mom and the detective. "Wonderful news. Thank you, JD." She gave Mom's hand a squeeze. "I have to get back up to the platform. It's time to open the dance floor." Her eyes sparkled as she glanced around the table. "I hope to see all of you dancing."

As Aunt Connie made her way back to the front, Mom sent Samantha a look. "I know you will be."

Bob and Mitzi were among the first to dance.

Soon others joined them.

When the band began to play *Unchained Melody*, JD leaned close to Mom. "Would you like to dance, Miz Carr?"

Samantha bit her lip to suppress a gasp. Her mother's expression was thoughtful. *Is she really considering it?*

After a brief pause, Mom gave Samantha's hand a gentle squeeze and smiled. "If you will stop calling me, Miz Carr. My name is Eva Grace."

Samantha sat back and looked at JD in complete wonder.

He stood and offered his hand. "Eva Grace, would you care to dance?"

Mom released Samantha's hand and pushed away from the table.

As the two made their way to the dance floor, Uncle Paul leaned in. "Are you in shock, Samantha?"

Samantha nodded. "I believe I am."

He chuckled as he pushed away from the table and turned to his daughter. "May I have this dance?"

Teagan's face lit as she left on her dad's arm.

Drew returned to Samantha's side and extended

his hand. "Shall we join them?"

Samantha gave a soft laugh as she rose. "I thought you'd never ask."

On the dance floor, he drew her close. "What a surprising night, huh?"

Samantha's gaze found her mother's. Mom's face reflected joy and something unexpected—peace. "More like shocking. I did not expect that."

"Neither did I, but they kind of go together, don't you think?"

She leaned back to look him in the eyes. "I'm open to the possibility."

He swung her around and then pulled her close again. "Are you open to the possibility of another date with me?"

She laid her head against his shoulder, inhaled the spicy scent of his cologne, and allowed her imagination to run off-leash.

"I am." *Most definitely, yes.*

The Visitor Catches the Bouquet

Preview by Marji Laine

"Miz Hawkins, have you seen my aunt?" MacKenzie Chastain peered into the kitchen as the woman stirred the glaze for the ham. She waltzed over to give the cook a half-hug.

"I spotted her coming in. Totin' a heavy bag from the looks of it. Just a bit ago, and I invited her to stow her gear in the volunteer office." The woman set her spoon down and reached to give Mac a kiss on the cheek. "She's prolly still there, chatting with Myron."

Mac thanked the sweet lady and made her way through the dining hall that was already filling with ornate structures in silver and blue. The Fashion Extravaganza tomorrow was bound to bring in plenty of funds to support Archway Kids for another year. It wouldn't have happened without Aunt Connie and support from The Wright Foundation. The Lord had brought so many amazing people into Mac's life for the celebrations this week. Especially Eric.

As though called by her thoughts, the man of her dreams rounded a corner from the activity center. "You seeing this?" He gestured to the artistic arch that spanned the stage area and touched the elevated ceiling.

She encircled her arms around his taut waist. "Marvelous, isn't it? When the lighting arrives, this little room will look like a Paris fashion salon."

"Our designer will certainly compare well." He kissed the top of her head. "I don't think we have to worry about that."

The invitation-only event had been sold out for over a week, and the tickets covered the cost of the decor and food. It would be the sales of the designs that made the difference. Mac could only hope that her brainchild would catapult Archway Kids to the next level of donations.

"Heading to the storage shed for more mirrors. The activity center isn't nearly as fancy as in here, but the tables are getting there." He gave her another squeeze and continued through the room.

She glanced up once more at the arch that would be the models' entrance and exit. The catwalk hadn't been constructed yet, but the effect would be elegant and professional when all was said and done. They would never have been able to swing this without the help and generosity of Alfred Rodan. His internationally-known fashions were sure to fetch high prices, both in the orders he would get both from the attending distributors and the silent auction for the modeled samples.

A mixture of anticipation and anxiety rippled across her shoulders.

No fear. This would succeed. It had to.

"Hey, kid." Her father's voice spun her around. "You're just the gal I needed." He held out a hand.

"What's up?" Her aunt would have to wait for a minute longer. She took Daddy's hand and followed him toward the front door.

"I want to make sure this is all right."

They stepped out the front door and into the fenced lot that they used as a playground for the after-school children. Only Dad had made it more of a fantasy land. Even in the sun, the twinkle lights shone from around the numerous trees and dangled between them. He'd set up benches, wicker chairs, and couches with tan cushions in small groupings among the trees. In the center of the lot, a lighted fountain glowed from an interior light that reflected the spray.

"Dad, this is beautiful. Like a fairyland."

"I'm glad you like it. I never counted myself as any kind of designer."

She held up her hands toward one of the groupings. Tasteful and elegant. "Clearly you were wrong." She pulled her phone out of her pocket. "Get closer, so I can commemorate this." The arrangements wouldn't last a week in this place when it was full of kids. "I want to remember how you have them, so we can duplicate the look for the next big event."

He smiled at her until her phone flashed.

"Cheesy grin, Dad."

"Well, don't you worry about all this." He widened his raised arm to take in the area. "I plan to have it all back to normal by Sunday night."

"Good, good. I'm on the hunt for Aunt Connie."

"Is she here?" Dad paused his adjusting of a string of lights draping from one of the trees.

"That's what I'm told. I'll find out." Mac opened the door and went back into the large building. "Now, where are you dear aunt o'mine?"

She made her way down the hall to a large room full of cabinets and tables that they all shared for office space. She pushed open the door. "Aunt Connie?"

"No Aunt Connie here." Myron Cassidy stood at the copier. "I'm making the programs." He handed her the pre-embossed card with the schedule on it. "You like?"

She glanced at the elegant lettering. "Nice." She handed it back to him. "I was looking for my aunt. Have you seen her?"

"No one's come in since I've been in here, but I think Trent's down in his office."

Great. She hadn't spotted the business manager and hoped that he would stay away from the event all together. Something about the bossy man rankled her and kept her on guard.

She made her way down to the small office that had been the director's office before Trent came. When the man had offered to straighten out their accounts, his one requirement was a place of his own to work. So, Mr. Hawkins had given up his space and now shared the community office with the rest of them. Thankfully, Trent would be gone soon, when The Wright Foundation formally put Archway

Kids under their prestigious banner. Until then, she planned to keep her distance from the man as much as possible.

Except in this case.

His door was slightly ajar, and she gave it a tap and nudged it full open. "Hi, Trent, I'm looking for my . . ." She stared at the woman on her knees behind the door. ". . . Aunt Connie."

"Call 9-1-1" Her dark-haired aunt looked up at her with a haunted expression.

Mac pulled her phone from her pocket and put in the call. "What's going on?"

Aunt Connie turned toward her. Blood covered her hands and streaked the side of her cheek. "I think he's dead."

Enjoy The Visitor's Next Trip

From the Story
Haven's Flight by Dena Netherton

How can you flee from an unseen enemy?

Haven Ellingsen enrolled in Life Ventures Therapy Camp in the Cascade Mountains to help her heal from horrible memories of her mother's violent death at the hands of an armed robber. But now, a greater fear dogs her steps. The rustle of leaves or the snap of a twig could be nothing. Or it might signal the sinister presence of the stalker who won't stop following her. It seems like a cruel trick from God to throw Haven into another dangerous situation only a year after her mom's murder.

He hides near her tent and listens to the girl talk with the counselor. Mostly she talks about her father. She's unhappy, and he can't stand to listen and do nothing about it. He needs to rescue her. He needs to make sure she doesn't ever go back to that man. His own father was the cause of his mother's death. And Ruth's. He can't let that happen again. Not with this girl. When the time is right, he'll make sure she'll be safe. And he will feel peace for the first time in years.

Can one month of survival training equip a girl to face all that the rugged wilderness and a madman can dish out?

Though the Sally Ingram Home of the Innocents is a fictional name, *Home of the Innocents* exists in Shelbyville, Kentucky, and most likely in your hometown or city also. According to their website, *Home of the Innocents* is busy "Providing residential and community services for medically complex children and families in the child welfare system." Of course, Aunt Connie Wright and the Wright Foundation would be drawn to such a worthy cause.

Acknowledgments

Well, here it is—my first cozy mystery. Thanks for including me, Marji Laine, of Write Integrity Press.

I thank God for His grace and forgiveness—the underlying theme of this story. I've been on the receiving end countless times. I'd also like to thank Marji Laine and Lillian Kohler for their help with editing and polishing the story. Thank you, Gail Johnson, and Kristy Horine, my faithful critiquers. You know me well and you always get my jokes.

I'm grateful and thankful for a loving family. You make it easy for me to write about loving families. Like the girl in this story, I have precious encouragers in my life that help keep my head on straight. Thank you, Cherry, Debbie, and Robin.

Thank you, readers, for your ongoing support of my efforts. I hope you enjoyed the story, and I pray that the message touches your heart and gives you the strength to forgive those who have wronged you.

It was for freedom that Christ set us free; therefore keep standing firm and do not be subject again to a yoke of slavery. – Galatians 5:1 NASB

About the Author

Betty Thomason Owens was born in an Army hospital in the Pacific Northwest but grew up in California, Tennessee, and Kentucky. An avid reader and storyteller from a young age, she didn't begin a writing career until her late thirties. In 2011, she attended a local writers conference where she was encouraged to continue writing. After self-publishing a couple of fantasy novels, she received a contract for her first historical romance series. Her stories often feature strong women dealing with difficult life situations. Many also contain an element of suspense.

Now a multi-published writer of historical romance, suspense, and fantasy fiction, she and her husband reside in Kentucky. They have three grown sons and seven grandchildren.

You can learn more about her at BettyThomasonOwens.com.

Connect with her on Facebook, Twitter, Pinterest, and Instagram.

Also By Betty

Latest Release:

Home Found Romantic Suspense

The Sins of the Father?
A car wreck, recurring nightmares, questions without answers...
Could all of this point to a forgotten past?

The Kinsman-Redeemer Series

The biblical saga of Ruth comes alive amid the racial tensions and quiet life of 1950 Tennessee.

The Legacy Series

Three generations of strong women, determined to succeed through the most turbulent of times.

Thank you
for reading our books!

Please consider leaving a review for the author
on the purchase page for this book.

Look for other books
published by

P

Pursued Books
an imprint of

W

Write Integrity Press
www.WriteIntegrity.com